Reading Toni Morrison's *Beloved*

Reading Toni Morrison's *Beloved*

A Literature Insight

by Paul McDonald

HEB ☼ Humanities-Ebooks, LLP

First published by *Humanities-Ebooks, LLP,*
Tirril Hall, Tirril, Penrith CA10 2JE

Cover image © Pamela Dumont

The Pdf Ebook is available to private purchasers from http://www.humanities-ebooks.co.uk and to libraries from Ebrary, EBSCO and MyiLibrary.com.

ISBN 978-1-84760-287-9 Pdf Ebook
ISBN 978-1-84760-327-2 Paperback
ISBN 978-1-84760-328-9 Kindle Ebook
ISBN 978-1-84760-329-6 ePub Ebook

Contents

1. Introduction

Toni Morrison's *Beloved* is one of the most successful novels of all time, selling millions of copies internationally and inspiring critical commentary from scholars of the highest distinction. Its influence is such that it is studied by students of literature around the world and is often cited as one of the most significant books of modern times. However, its popularity belies its difficulty: many find the novel hard to read, struggling with its structure and occasionally fragmented style. This guide is designed to help readers engage with this complex book and achieve a deeper understanding of its context, the literary strategies it employs, and the various ways in which it has been interpreted since its publication in 1987.

The book has been seen as both modernist and postmodernist in its form and philosophy. Its disorientating narrative strategy is occasionally reminiscent of those modernist writers who stress the fragmented nature of experience, while its subversive approach to history asserts a fictional past that is characteristically postmodern. At the same time *Beloved* can also be seen as a work of scrupulous realism, painstakingly researched; and while it is occasionally described as magic realist, the author is careful to offer a non-supernatural explanation for the appearance of her otherworldly eponymous character. Such issues have preoccupied critics since the novel was published and this guide addresses them, showing how they relate to the text's primary themes of racism, motherhood, language, and history's bearing on the present. Morrison's African American heritage is central to this and informs the book's representation of the world at every level. Its attitude to the past is distinctly African American, for instance, as concepts like 'rememory' attest. Likewise African American traditions influence the book's style with its use of call-and-response structures, its tolerance of ambiguity and openness, and its affinities with jazz music and black oral culture. *Beloved* offers few answers to the questions it addresses, putting the onus of interpretation on the reader, but it is impossible to engage fully with the novel without an understanding of those questions: this guide ensures that readers can appreciate them, and thus fully benefit from Morrison's extraordinary achievement.

2. Biographical and Social Context

2.1 Morrison before Beloved.

Toni Morrison was born Chloe Ardelia Wofford in Lorain, Ohio in 1931. Her parents were Southerners who migrated north to Ohio in the early twentieth century, and this is where Morrison spent her youth. She attended Lorain High School where she was an honours student, developing a love of the classics of European literature from Jane Austen to Dostoevsky; at the same time her home life inspired a fondness for less formal storytelling, including traditional tales from non-western oral culture: her feel for spoken language would go on to have a significant influence on the character and complexion of Morrison's writing.

Toni Morrison became a Catholic at the age of 12 and took the confirmation name Anthony, changing this to Toni because people kept mispronouncing it.[1] Her interest in religion at this early age is indicative of a serious mind, and she was intelligent too: when she entered Howard University she was the first member of her family to attend college. She majored in English with a classics minor, graduating with a BA in 1953. She followed this with an MA in English from Cornell University, her thesis focusing on the theme of alienation and death in the work of Virginia Woof and William Faulkner. The unconventional narrative strategies of such writers have a bearing on Morrison's own style as will be seen later. After graduating from Cornell in 1955, Morrison spent some time as a teacher, first at Texas Southern University, then at the University of Houston. In 1958 she married the Jamaican architect, Howard Morrison. The marriage produced two children, Harold Ford Morrison (1961) and Slade Kevin Morrison (1964), but ended in divorce in 1964. It seems

---

1 Toni Morrison: 'I want to feel what I feel. Even if it's not happiness' Interview with Emma Brockes. *The Guardian*, Friday 13 April 2012. See online sources.

that there were unbridgeable cultural differences between Morrison and her husband: his attitude to women appears to have been rather backward-looking, and this clashed with Morrison's independence. In order to escape the pressure of marriage and domesticity Morrison began attending a creative writing group, and this was an important move: though she initially had no plans to become an author, the group stimulated her interest in writing; at first she shared material that she had written at college, but gradually went on to create original stories for the group, some of which found their way into her later fiction. Her interest in writing took a slightly different course in 1965 when she responded to an advert she saw for a job as a textbook editor. Despite being a single mother with two children she took the huge step of giving up full time teaching to pursue a career as an editor, first at a subsidiary of Random House in Syracuse, New York; then from 1967 as a senior editor at the Random House city headquarters.

In the late 60s Morrison began work on her first novel, *The Bluest Eye*, which after a number of rejections was eventually published in 1970. The novel grew out of a short story she had originally written for her writing group some years earlier. Told in both the first and third person, the plot concerns an eleven year old African American girl, Pecola Breedlove, who, feeling inferior because of her looks, yearns for blue eyes and a white complexion. Set in Morrison's home town of Lorain in 1941, it is partly about black identity and the problems of achieving self-respect in the face of conventional notions of beauty: Pecola goes insane as a result of her quest for beauty, and the novel ends with her imagining that she actually *does* have the blue eyes that she desires. The story is markedly unsettling in parts—at one point Pecola is raped by her drunken father—and it attracted much controversy as a result; there have even been attempts to ban it from schools in the States. Many critics praised the sensitivity with which Pecola is depicted, however, and the astonishing lyricism of Morrison's prose. While the novel was not commercially successful, it was clear to most reviewers that it marked the arrival of a major talent.

Morrison achieved an important and influential position as an editor at Random House, one of the first black people to occupy such a job at a major publishing house. In her time as an editor she played a central role in editing and championing black writers such as the poet and story writer Henry Dumas (1934–1968), and the activist Angela Davis (b. 1944), as well as working on books for celebrity figures like Mohammed Ali. In addition, because of the critical success of *The Bluest Eye,* journals began to look to her as a spokesperson on black writing and culture, and she published numerous reviews and articles on the topic. Thus increasingly Morrison began to occupy a significant role in African American culture.

In 1974 Morrison took on a project called *The Black Book*, a collection of documents by African American people designed to deepen understanding of their history. While researching it Morrison came across the story of Margaret Garner, an escaped slave from Kentucky who, when she was eventually caught in Cincinnati, attempted to kill her four children rather than see them committed to slavery. She only succeeded in killing one: a daughter. The story was very high profile in the mid-nineteenth century and became a focus for abolitionists who used the case to foreground the horrors of slavery; years later it would become the inspiration for *Beloved.*

Morrison was a devoted and talented editor, but alongside her career she also found time to further develop her own writing, publishing *Sula* in 1973, and *The Song of Solomon* in 1977. *Sula* generated even more critical attention than *The Bluest Eye* and is a story about two black women with different upbringings: the conservative Nel, and the less conventional Sula, both of whom reside in the small town of Bottom. While Nel marries and pursues a conventional life, Sula asserts her independence and leaves town, returning years later amid rumours of sexual excess and affairs with white men. Sula is criticised by the townsfolk, and by Nel too when her old friend has an affair with her husband. The novel is interesting for many reasons, not least because it challenges notions of convention, particularly regarding sexual relationships and female lifestyle. Morrison's third novel, *The Song of Solomon,* was more popular still, and is her first written from a male perspective. It is the story of Macon Dead III, nicknamed Milkman because he was breastfed past an appropriate age. He begins life as selfish, self-pitying individual, disengaged from the African American community. He is alienated at school, but loved by his family who do their best to engage with him despite the fact that he ignores them and becomes actively antisocial. As his complicated family history is revealed we see that his problems are partly associated with slavery and the extent to which his ancestors were abused. While he begins as a defeatist and heartless individual, Milkman eventually achieves a degree of insight and moral and emotional maturation, particularly as he comes to understand his family more fully. A few critics, including some of international repute like Harold Bloom, consider *The Song of Solomon* to be Morrison's best novel.

Both *Sula* and *The Song of Solomon* augmented Morrison's critical reputation hugely: the former was nominated for the American Book Award, and won the Ohioana Award, while the latter was chosen as a Book-of-the-Month-Club-Selection, and received the National Book Critics Circle Award, among many others. These novels established Morrison as a major figure in American letters, then, and in 1980 President Carter appointed her to the National Council on the Arts. When *Tar Baby* was published in 1981, Morrison appeared on the cover of *Newsweek*, the only other black woman to do so since the renowned novelist Zora Neale Hurston in 1943. *Tar Baby* is the story the relationship between Jadine and Son: a Sorbonne educated woman, and an impoverished man. Jadine's education has been funded by a wealthy white family, the Streets, and Son's arrival in her life challenges assumptions about the authority wealth creates in society. It is also about attitudes to race, and it picks up on the issues raised by the black power movement in the 60s and 70s. The latter advocated active and aggressive assertion of black rights, and these views are embodied to some degree by Son, a militant character who is outraged by Jardine's willingness to engage with white culture. The novel ends on an ambivalent note: while Son's radical views seem to have softened, the reader can't say if this extends to him pursuing a relationship with Jardine, which would signal a willingness to engage with white society.

Two years after the publication of *Tar Baby* Morrison gave up her job at Random House to take up take up a professorship at the State University of New York at Albany. In 1986 Morrison made her first foray into drama with a play commissioned by the New York State Writers Institute: *Dreaming Emmett* was based on the murder of a fourteen year old boy who was lynched in Mississippi for whistling at a white woman; though it is yet to appear in print, the play won the New York State Governor's Art Award when it was performed in the 1980s; as with *Beloved*, it is an example of Morrison using an historical event as a way into fiction.

So Morrison was a high profile and celebrated author by the time she began work on *Beloved* in the 1980s, but it was the publication of this, her fifth novel, which would make her an internationally renowned writer.

2.2 The Publication of Beloved.

In 1987, almost twenty years after Morrison came across the story of Margaret Garner, *Beloved* was published. Though she was inspired by this story, Morrison had no interest in documenting Garner's life literally. Rather she wanted to use it as a starting point for exploring the experience of someone like Garner, and the lives of people who have for the most part been omitted from history; her purpose, among other things, was to show the lives of slaves and ex-slaves from their perspective, rendering the story from within. She wanted, in other words, to personalise history by attaching it to the preoccupations and feelings of her characters.

Morrison strives to show rather than tell both in an artistic sense and in a moral sense: she wants us to feel the experiences of the ex-slaves, but also wants us to engage with Sethe's decision to kill her baby and assess it for ourselves. She doesn't steer us morally, claiming that she felt unable to ethically evaluate the act of infanticide herself: 'there is no one qualified who can,' she says 'except the child itself.'[1] Certainly it was a struggle for Morrison to create the book, more so than any of her previous novels. As she says in one interview:

1 'A Bench by the Road: *Beloved* by Toni Morrison.' In Denard, C. Carolyn (ed.). *Toni Morrison: Conversations.* (Mississippi: University Press of Mississippi, 2008) 44–50. 46

> For *Beloved* […] there was almost nothing that I knew that I
> seemed sure of, nothing I could really use. All of my books have
> been different for me, but *Beloved* was like I'd never written a
> book before. It was brand new […] I thought, more than I've
> thought about any book, 'I cannot do this.' I thought that a lot.
> And I stopped for long, long, long periods of time and said, 'I
> know I've never read a book like this because who can write it?'
> But then I decided that was a very selfish way to think. After all,
> these people had lived that life. This book was only a tiny little
> part of what some of that life had been. If all I had to do was sit
> in a room and look at paper and imagine it, then it seemed a little
> vain and adolescent for me to complain about the difficulty of
> that work. I was also pricked by the notion that the institution,
> which had been so organized and had lasted so long, was beyond
> art. And that depressed me so much that I would just write some
> more [Morrison in Denard, 49]

Beloved didn't come easily for Morrison, then, partly because of the
strain it put on her imagination, and partly because it was emotionally draining. It is clear, however, that she felt a moral duty of sorts to
produce it. She has a sense that it might not even be possible to write
about slavery, but felt compelled to because she felt so strongly that
the subject needed to be addressed.

Originally Morrison conceived of *Beloved* as a much longer work,
and when she first gave the manuscript to her editor it was on the
assumption that she was submitting a draft of a story that would be
triple the length. Her editor convinced her that what she had written so far constituted a book in itself,[1] but later Morrison produced
two more novels, *Jazz* (1992) and *Paradise* (1997), which extend the
project and which together with *Beloved* constitute a trilogy.

Beloved was spectacularly successful, selling out its initial print
run of 100,000 copies and reaching the *New York Times* bestseller
list almost immediately. It went on to create an international reputation for Toni Morrison, winning the Anisfield Wolf Book Award in
Race Relations, the Melcher Book Award, and the American Book

---

1   Ellyn Sanna 'Biography of Toni Morrison.' Bloom, Harold (ed). *Toni Morrison*
(Philadelphia: Chelsea House Publishers, 2002) 3–39. 4

Award; indeed there were remonstrations when it did not also win the National Book Award: 48 black writers and critics put their names to a protest in *The New York Times Book Review*, arguing that it should also be a contender for the Pulitzer Prize, which it did go on to win in 1988, together with the Robert F. Kennedy Book Award and the Elmer Holmes Bobst Award for Fiction. Morrison has also had a very high profile supporter in Oprah Winfrey who selected a number of her books, including *Beloved*, for the influential Oprah's Book Club, guaranteeing massive commercial success. In 1998 Winfrey produced and starred in a film version of *Beloved*, which naturally brought the novel to the attention of an even larger global audience.

2.3 Morrison after Beloved

In 1992 Morrison published a collection of critical essays: *Playing in the Dark: Whiteness and the Literary Imagination* (1992), and an edited collection, *Race-ing Justice, En-gendering Power: Essays on Anita Hill, Clarence Thomas, and the Construction of Social Reality* (1992). Her literary criticism is particularly interesting, and offers a rereading of some the key books in the American literary canon. Among other things it aims to show how so-called classic texts respond to the presence of Africans and African Americans: she reveals how the white imagination has been shaped by black experiences, and argues that it is misguided to think that classic white American literature might be in any way free of black influence.

Her next novel, *Jazz*, also appeared in 1992, and is seen as the second instalment of a trilogy of novels that started with *Beloved* and ends with *Paradise* in 1997. *Jazz* begins at the height of the so-called Jazz Age (the 1920s), and focuses on the next generation to Sethe and Paul D, and their grandchildren. It features Joe and Violet Trace who are indicative of those many black people who migrated North from the South in the late nineteenth and early twentieth century. Joe shoots his young girlfriend, Dorcas, who allows herself to bleed to death rather that reveal that Joe was her attacker: like Sethe she loves someone more than she loves herself, and as a whole the book deals with similar themes of identity and the disintegration of the self. The third installment of the trilogy, *Paradise,* focuses on more recent black history. It is set in the 60s and 70s, and the title reflects its interest in the notion of utopia and how this relates to race and gender. It depicts the all-Black town of Ruby, Oklahoma, and a group of women who live together in a nearby mansion known as the Convent. When the town goes into decline the women of the Convent are scapegoated and massacred by the men of Ruby. It is impossible to know the race of the Convent women and they are blamed not because of who they are but of what they represent for their attackers: as Shirley Ann Stave suggests, 'the Convent [...] haunts the community precisely because the fears and psychic wounds that they [the town] brought with them get mapped onto [...] the women of the Convent.'[1] Just like the characters of *Beloved*, the men of Ruby are haunted by their past, and the town's history of being founded by former slaves. The townsfolk are on a doomed mission to keep Ruby pure: it is a folly because an insistence on purity precludes a healthy engagement with the world, invariably precipitating the persecution of innocents.

Though undoubtedly powerful and significant novels, neither *Jazz* nor *Paradise* were as successful as *Beloved*, and to a greater or lesser extent this has been the case with Morrison's later fiction, including *Love* (2003), *A Mercy* (2008), and *Home* (2012). Still, the critical consensus is that all of Morrison's novels are worthy of attention, and she is yet to write a bad novel as such. Certainly Morrison's place as an author on the world stage was assured when in 1993 she won the Nobel Prize, and in 2006 *Beloved* was chosen as Best Work of American Fiction in the Last 25 Years by the *New York Times*.

Morrison remains a figure of global significance, and her reputation is not just based on *Beloved*, or indeed solely on her work as a novelist. Not only is she a spokesperson for black issues, she is remarkably diverse creatively: she wrote the lyrics for a cycle of songs commissioned by Carnegie Hall in 1993, collaborating with Andre Previn, and has co-authored a series of children's books with

---

1   Shirley Ann Stave. 'Jazz and Paradise: Pivotal Moments in Black History.' In Tally, Justine (ed). *The Cambridge Companion to Toni Morrison*. (Cambridge: Cambridge University Press, 2007) 59–75. 69.

her son Slade Morrison, the first of which, *The Big Box* appeared in 1999. She wrote the libretto for an opera, *Margaret Garner*, a collaboration with the composer Richard Danielpour, which was first performed in 2005. In 2006 she curated 'A Foreigner's Home' exhibition at the Louvre in Paris, and in 2011 she created *Desdemona*, a collaboration with opera director Peter Sellars and songwriter Rokia Traoré: the project gives a posthumous voice to the murdered character of Desdemona in Shakespeare's *Othello*, and explores her relationship with her African nurse, Barbary. Thus Morrison's creative drive appears undiminished even in her 80s, and her latest novel *Home* received enough plaudits to suggest that her powers as a novelist remain strong.

3. Literary Strategies

3.1 Magic Realism

A term that is often applied to *Beloved* is magic realism which, according to the British critic David Lodge, applies to fiction 'when marvellous and impossible events occur in what otherwise purports to be realistic narrative.'[1] Lodge associates it with writing about issues that are somehow too difficult to address in conventional, 'undisturbed' realism, observing that many employ it to depict profound personal or social trauma. Lodge also notes that magic realism appears to lend itself to the treatment of subjects that defy logic or that seem too horrendous to tackle in a straightforward way. Magic realism seems right for a subject such as the Holocaust, for instance, as can be seen in the work of writers like Jonathan Safran Foer, David Grossman, and D. M. Thomas; or for the absurdities of totalitarianism notable in the writing of Milan Kundera. Similarly the nature of Morrison's subject in *Beloved* seems appropriate for a ghost story: what better way of exploring a trauma that won't die but which needs to be dealt with? Indeed, what better way of addressing a subject that seems impossible to square with our understanding of how our fellow human beings should be treated? In a sense Morrison uses something beyond belief in Western culture, a haunting, to represent something else that seems beyond belief in the modern world: the institution of slavery.

Magic realism features more in some countries' literary histories than others, and this might in part have to do with differing cultural attitudes to magic. In some cultures distinctions between reality and the supernatural are less well defined than in others. African culture is one that embraces magic, for instance, and such traditions and attitudes also became part of African American culture. As Morrison suggests:

---

1   David Lodge. *The Art of Fiction*. (London: Penguin, 1992) 114

> We are a very practical people, very down to earth, even shrewd people. But within that practicality we also accepted what I suppose could be called superstition and magic, which is another way of knowing things. But to blend those two worlds together at the same time was enhancing, not limiting. And some of those things were 'discredited knowledge' that Black people had; discredited only because Black people were discredited and therefore what they knew was 'discredited.'[1]

Morrison herself was raised in a family that had some feeling for the supernatural. Many of the tales she heard as a child were ghost stories, for instance, and her parents and grandparents had a belief in the spirit world. For Morrison so-called magic and superstition seems to offer an additional way of understanding that does not necessarily negate conventional ways of thinking, but complements, and even augments them. Morrison feels that magic and superstition were 'discredited' because they are associated with black people; black people were considered inferior as a race and so their culture and philosophy were dismissed by extension. This dismissal also has to do with the fact that the supernatural cannot be reconciled with post-Enlightenment rationalism and the kind of assumptions that inform Western thinking. The Enlightenment privileged reason and because this cannot account for magic it has a history of being rejected and ridiculed in the West.

Where realism is compatible with Western thought, then, magic is not. In terms of the relationship between Africa and the West, there is a sense in which these terms and the ways of thinking they represent also have a political dimension. Historically Western imperialist powers had an essentialist, universal view of their ideas and values: colonial powers assumed there is one way of doing and seeing things, and sought to impose those views on cultures across the world. Western thought—based on science, logic and reason—was privileged at the expense of other ways of thinking and this became a facet of the subaltern's exclusion or oppression. Though America is a post-colonial nation, having liberated itself from British rule in the eight-

---

1   Toni Morrison, "Rootedness: The Ancestor as Foundation," in *Black Women Writers (1950–1980)*, ed. Mari Evans (New York: Doubleday, 1983), 342.

eenth century, it is still associated with colonial attitudes and modes of colonial tyranny (of which slavery is an example). In modern postcolonial writing the magical can be a way of challenging that tyranny; it can be employed to interrogate that history of exclusion. To some extent this is Morrison's purpose in *Beloved*. For Morrison it becomes a way of reclaiming history, as Mehri Razmi and Leyli Jamali suggest:

> Applying postcolonial terminology, realism represents the hege-monic discourse of the colonizer while magic refers to the strat-egy of opposition and resistance used by the colonized. Magical realism can also provide a way to fill in the gaps of cultural rep-resentation in a postcolonial context by recovering the fragments and voices of forgotten histories from the point of view of the colonized.[1]

The magical elements of a text like *Beloved* offer an implicit chal-lenge to the dominant modes of thinking, and a way of exploring aspects of the black experience that have previously been supressed or overlooked. One example of this is how Morrison uses *Beloved* to explore the forgotten history of the Middle Passage, which is a term used to describe the transportation of Africans to their place of enslavement:

> Introducing a magical character with a narrative voice, *Beloved* distorts the traditional conception of reality accord-ing to Eurocentric definitions. Moreover, *Beloved* becomes the medium through which victims of the Middle Passage gain a literate voice. This functions as a narrative strategy of transgres-sion since it allows for the voices of the under- or un-represented. In this way *Beloved* can be understood as a writing back from the periphery. [Mehri Razmi and Leyli Jamali, 118]

The Middle Passage experience in African American history is under-represented and Morrison uses her ghost character to remedy this shortcoming: as some see it, Beloved (the character) becomes a vehicle for collective memory in the book, magically transformed

---

1   Mehri Razmi and Leyli Jamali, 'Magic(al) Realism as Postcolonial Device in Toni Morrison's *Beloved*. *International Journal of Humanities and Social Science* Vol. 2 No. 5; March 2012. 111–119. 112

into someone who witnesses and articulates the horror of a slave ship crossing, her story filling some of the gaps that realism has left. As a magical character Beloved can be more than one thing: she is a murdered daughter, a bereaved daughter, a captured slave, an abused woman, ghost and a corporeal being; she is simultaneously dead and alive, rather like the traumatic history she symbolises: just as the Middle Passage is a fact of history that is inadequately remembered, so Beloved is a phenomenon that the Cincinnati community has practically forgotten by the close of the story.

So the magical elements of *Beloved* can be seen as a political as well as a literary strategy when viewed in the context of black people's history of oppression and marginalization.

3.2 Call and Response Structures

Morrison suggests that she was looking to embrace a black aesthetic in *Beloved* and employ storytelling strategies characteristic of those associated with black culture. In one interview she says:

> If my work is faithfully to reflect the aesthetic tradition of Afro-American culture, it must make conscious use of the characteristics of its art forms and translate them into print: antiphony, the group nature of art, its functionality, its improvisational nature, its relationship to audience performance.[1]

As Maggie Sale has noted, the traits she lists here are those related to African American oral culture; among other things this involves the idea of art as an interactive, community experience that can be made in the moment, rather than the more Western idea of art as something that is fixed and which originates with a single person. In particular Sale sees antiphony—the call and response pattern—as central to *Beloved*. The call and response form has African American roots, developing 'in spirituals and play and work songs' [Sale, 178] and is characterised by interaction between voices: a speaker makes a statement and the listener replies to that statement, and the topic

---

1   Maggie Sale 'Call and Response as Critical Method: African–American Oral Traditions and *Beloved*' In Solomon, Barbara H. *Critical Essays on Toni Morrison's* Beloved. (New York: G.K. Hall & Co, 1998) 177–188. 177

evolves as a sort of drama with both speaker and listener influencing its development. There is also a sense in which the nature of what is said is shaped to fit the context and the needs of both parties: the nature of the call is influenced by the moment, and the response is subjective depending on the character and circumstances of those who respond. Art produced in this way acknowledges the importance of dialogue, and considers meaning as something that has the potential to change. There is a call and response structure to Baby Suggs's orations in the Clearing of course: she does not like to think of these as sermons because she feels she is too ignorant to sermonize; rather she would put out a call: 'she called and the hearing heard' [Sale, 177]. Sale notes also that in *Beloved* stories of the past allow for competing versions to exist simultaneously; they too have a call and response structure:

> Within the novel, individual (hi)stories are told, listened to, and believed depending upon the relationship between teller and listener. Similarly, these individual (hi)stories combine to create the text of *Beloved*, whose (hi)story as a whole is told (written), listened to (read), and believed depending upon the relation between teller (writer) and listener (reader) [Sale 179].

Sale also sees a call and response pattern in Sethe and Beloved's relationship: Sethe's guilt calls Beloved back from the dead and when she returns Beloved calls on Sethe to answer for the act of taking her life, and Sethe responds. Similarly, Denver calls on the women of the community to help at the end of the story, and they respond by answering and uniting to exorcise Beloved. Patterns of this kind feature throughout the book, and a good example of how it works between characters can be seen in the way Denver's birth is narrated. All Denver has to go on for her understanding of this event is Sethe's memory of what happened: when Sethe told the story to Denver she emphasised certain things such as the theft of her milk because they were the most important aspects for her. However when Denver tells the same story she focuses more on the role of Amy–Denver. In other words different aspects of the story are privileged depending on the needs of the teller, and such privileging changes the story. Tales are also shaped by the needs of the listener, which is evident when Denver tells Beloved the same story. There is a sense in which the Denver and Beloved create the story together in order to fulfil their individual needs. Denver is desperate to entertain Beloved ('to construct out of the strings she has heard all her life a net to hold Beloved'), while Beloved craves information about Sethe to feed her obsession with the woman she believes is her mother:

> The monologue became [...] a duet as they lay down together, Denver nursing Beloved's interest like a lover whose pleasure was to over-feed the loved [...] Denver spoke, Beloved listened, and the two did the best they could to create what really happened, how it really was, something only Sethe knew because she alone had the mind for it and the time afterward to shape it: the quality of Amy's voice, her breath like burning wood [quoted in Sale, 183].

What they create together is essentially a fiction (given that the truth is 'something only Sethe knew'), but it serves the needs of each individual. This reconstruction of history is emblematic of how history is presented in the novel as a whole: it is a dialogue, a call and response created out of a variety of voices that precludes the possibility of a single truth.

The call and response structure in *Beloved* is one that refuses to resolve issues, and in this sense the reader must engage creatively with the narrative, offering their individual subjective responses and making sense of the text in their own way. Lots of things are left unresolved in the book: characters disappear from the story never to return, and some scenes—such as the Middle Passage chapters—are deliberately fragmented and irreducible. At the end of the novel the fate of Beloved herself becomes a mystery for the reader to solve: the book calls on the reader to make a response, and the nature of such responses will be different depending on the reader's point of view.

The reader's creative role also has particular significance in relation to the issue of morality. The act of killing a baby to save her from slavery is a morally complex one of course: on the one hand, praising Sethe for having the courage to make a stand on behalf of liberty denies the child's right to life; on the other, condemning Sethe unequivocally ignores the validity of the mother's love for her daughter.

However, Morrison creates a space in which various views on this can exist side by side. Baby Suggs, schoolteacher, and Stamp Paid all offer perspectives on Sethe's act before we are presented with Sethe's version. All versions of the event differ and no one version can be called the truth, not even Sethe's. One reason why we do not receive the truth from Sethe is that she finds it impossible to convey the experience in anything other than a roundabout and incomplete way. When she tries to communicate it to Paul D she can only offer fragments and hope he'll understand; but she comes to see that he never will. All she can do as she tries to tell him is circle around the issue, a notion underscored in the book by the fact that Sethe is literally circling the room:

> Sethe knew that the circle she was making around the room, him, the subject, would remain one. That she could never close in, pin it down for anybody who had to ask. If they didn't get it right off—she could never explain [quoted in Sale, 184]

Sethe has a perspective that no one can share, and any responses she gets to any call she makes on this issue may never match her needs. Paul D cannot see it her way, Baby Suggs cannot see it her way, and the reader may not either. So Morrison does not privilege Sethe's position, and does not answer the question of why she killed her child. As Sale says, 'The novel's structure [...] insists that readers move among positions and inhabit multiple perspectives [Sale 184]. This call and response method creates a narrative that is more meaningful than any single perspective could be, even though it cannot be considered true, or the final world: each call—i.e. each question it poses—anticipates and makes space for a different subjective response.

3.3 Beloved and the Jazz Aesthetic

The call and response pattern is central to African American music and many critics have noted the affinities between *Beloved*'s narrative and musical forms such as jazz. Some of the technical parallels with jazz include antiphony, repetition, theme and variation, and a tolerance of openness. For instance, the musical nature of the call and response pattern can be seen in Baby Suggs's sermon; as Lars Eckstein notes it 'evokes the Afro-Christian tradition of sermonising and singing. Her "call" in the Clearing adheres to the typical features of antiphonic sermonising.'[1] Consider this extract:

> In this here place, we flesh; flesh that weeps, laughs; flesh that dances on bare feet in grass. Love it. Love it hard. Yonder they do not love your flesh. They despise it. They don't love your eyes; they'd just as soon pick em out. No more do they love the skin on your back. Yonder they flay it. And O my people they do not love your hands. [Quoted in Eckstein , 274]

This has a rhythmic structure and uses sound patterning to create its effects. Note the repetition of words like flesh and love; it seems to gather in impetus and intensity as it unfolds, and as in Afro-Christian sermons there is a crescendo effect.

Similarly Cheryll Hall demonstrates how much the repetition in *Beloved*'s narrative is reminiscent of jazz. Scenes like Denver's birth and Sethe's abuse at the hands of schoolteacher are reiterated from various points of view, a technique akin to the 'theme and variation movement between voices and instruments in jazz.'[2] There are also repeated motifs in *Beloved* too, such as Paul D.'s tobacco tin, and the various references to trees that punctuate the novel. Sometimes such motifs function merely as what Hall calls 'grace notes' and have little more than a pleasing 'ornamental' status, but sometimes they have powerful symbolic import; either way they function the way such repetitions function in jazz: 'the tiny shock of recognition we receive with each recurrent motif is akin to the pleasure we derive from identifying familiar phrases in complex jazz performance' [Hall, 93]. Hall also identifies elements in *Beloved* which have affinities with jazz jam sessions. Jam sessions are those in which musicians come together to produce one-off performances characterised by improvised solos and riffs [loose musical phrases recurring over changing melodies] repeated with variation and progression. They gener-

---

1   Lars Eckstein 'Love Supreme: Jazzthetic Strategies in Toni Morrison's *Beloved*. *African American Review*, 40, 2, 2006. 271–283. 274
2   Cheryll Hall '"Literary Habit": Oral Tradition and Jazz in Beloved. *Melus*, 19,1, 1994. 89–95. 92

ally end with musicians uniting to merge their 'solo efforts in what can be, to the uninitiated, a complex cacophony of sound' [Hall, 94]. Chapters twenty to twenty three of *Beloved* exhibit a similar spirit of jazz jamming. They are linked by the opening lines: 'Beloved, she my daughter. She mine.'; 'Beloved is my sister. I swallowed her blood right along with my mother's milk.'; 'I am Beloved and she is mine' [Quoted in Hall, 94]. Each chapter is characterised by a different voice: first Sethe, then Denver, and then two chapters from Beloved. In each case the soloist follows the lead of the previous 'performer', offering variations on the theme of rediscovering lost relatives. The 'voices are integrated after Beloved's second solo performance,' ultimately achieving an 'urgent polyphony' which culminates in the repetition of 'You are mine' at the end of chapter twenty three.

Occasionally Morrison's work is accused of ambiguity, and indeed there is much in *Beloved* that might be seen as unresolved and fragmentary: she rarely fills in gaps for the reader and this is suggestive of African American music too, as Morrison herself suggests in interview:

> I don't want them [the novels] to be unsatisfying, and some people do find it wholly unsatisfying, but I think that's the habit, the literary habit, of having certain kinds of endings. Although we don't expect a poem to end that way, you know, or even music doesn't end that way, certain kinds of music. There's always something tasty in your mouth when you hear blues, there's always something left over with jazz, because it's on edge, and you're never satisfied, you're always a little hungry [quoted in Hall 89].

Notice how she draws a direct parallel between writing and music, and particularly black musical forms like blues and jazz. What she approves of in jazz is the form's willingness to tolerate a lack of completion. She likes the fact that loose ends are part of the jazz aesthetic; they are part of hers too: the ambiguities that run throughout *Beloved*, particularly those associated with the title character, are sustained throughout, leaving the reader hungry and stimulated by the prospect of more. Again this is at odds with more conventional storytelling forms such as traditional realism which tend to be more struc- tured around a beginning, middle and end, and hence more predict- able. The jazz feel that people tend to perceive in Morrison's writing also makes critics want to place her in modernist tradition as will be seen later.

One critic, Paul Gilroy, argues that black music is inherently com- municative and has a symbolic import born of its cultural associ- ations; it captures something distinctive and essential in African American identity, constituting

> a place in which black vernacular has been able to preserve and cultivate both the distinctive rapport with the presence of death which derives from slavery and a related ontological state that I want to call the condition of pain [Quoted in Eckstein , 273]

For Gilroy there is a sense in which black people's history of suffering registers in black music; it conveys a 'condition of pain.' It is appro- priate that a novel about the horrors of slavery should embrace such musical structures, then, both at the level of symbolism and form. For the characters of *Beloved* there is sometimes a sense in which music can say what words cannot, and this has to do with music's ability to communicate the trauma of their experience: its otherwise inexpress- ible pain. When Sethe asks Paul D about his past, for instance, he says: 'I don't know. I never have talked about it. Not to a soul. Sang it sometimes, but never told a soul.'[1]

3.4 Free Indirect Discourse

The story of *Beloved* is told by a third person, omniscient narrator; in other words by an 'all-seeing' narrator who potentially knows every- thing about the story and can move in and out of characters' minds, and backwards and forwards in time as necessary. In some omnis- cient narratives it is easy to distinguish between the narrator's voice and the character's voices, mainly because the latter are bracket off from the narrator's voice with quotation marks and/or phrases like s/he said, s/he thought, s/felt, and so on. When quotation marks are

---

1   Toni Morrison, *Beloved*, (London: Picador, 1988. First published, 1987) 71. All future references to the novel will be made in the text.

used this is known as direct discourse, and when they are not used it is called indirect discourse. However sometimes narratives can blur the distinctions between a narrator's voice and a character's voice: this happens when the narrator adopts the tone and speech patterns of a particular character, and the narrative seems to shape itself around that character. *Beloved* does this a lot. Consider this passage that comes just after Sethe has revealed the truth about killing her baby to Paul D:

> The roaring in Paul D's head did not prevent him from hearing the pat she gave to the last word, and it occurred to him that what she wanted for her children was exactly what was missing from 124: safety.

This is told from Paul D's perspective, but it seems like the narrator's voice rather than Paul D's: it is rather neutral in tone, and descriptive. However, notice how the voice changes as the paragraph develops and the impact of Sethe's revelation begins to register with him:

> This here Sethe was new. The ghost in her house did not bother her for the very same reason a room–and board witch with new shoes was welcome. This here Sethe talked about love like any other woman; talked about the baby clothes like any other woman, but what she meant could cleave the bone. This here Sethe talked about safety with a handsaw. This here new Sethe didn't know where the world stopped and she began. [164]

This is still an omniscient third person narrator, of course, but notice how the narrator's voice seems to merge with Paul D's. There are no 'he thought' or 'he felt' tags, but his speech patterns are suggested by colloquial phrasing such as 'This here Sethe.' This kind of narrative technique is called Free Indirect Discourse. It is more common in modern novels than in earlier examples of the form, and this is often said to have something to do with a move away from moral certainty toward a more relativistic conception of morality. It the modern world people are less willing to think of moral issues in reductive, black and white terms. Because Paul's thoughts and opinions are not obviously set apart from the narrator's it is difficult to know where one ends and other begins: Paul D's views occupy the same level as the narrator's 'authoritative' voice and this gives them a weight that they might not have were they bracketed off as in much traditional realism; however, because they seem to belong to a character rather than the narrator, those views are not endorsed or privileged by the narrator either. The murder of Beloved is an issue of extreme moral complexity, and free indirect discourse is a narrative strategy that allows for a play of voices and opinions to exist alongside one another in a non-hierarchical way.

4. Sequential Development and Analysis

4.1 Chapter One

The first chapter of *Beloved* locates the story very specifically in time and place. As the novel progresses we get lots of flashbacks to earlier times and different places, but the principal 'now' and 'where' of the tale is made clear at the outset: it is 1873 in Cincinnati, Ohio. It is set during a period of American history called era of Reconstruction which refers to a time after the Civil War (1861–1865) when the American government sought to help the Southern states recover from the conflict and integrate with the North. The hope was to fully bring an end to the inequities of slavery by introducing reforms that would ensure equality. In the novel the notion of reconstruction also refers to the psychological state of African American peoples' struggle to rebuild themselves after the trauma of slavery; the idea of reconstruction extends to the ex-slaves' psychological rebuilding, which is a necessary process if they are to have a meaningful future.

A general point worth making at the outset is that the novel does not include many signposts to help orientate the reader: characters are introduced without too much explanation, and scenes and flash-backs aren't always fully contextualised. The narrative is convoluted and repetitious, full of ellipses and changes in direction. As a result *Beloved* is difficult to read, particularly at the outset, and arguably it is only by the end of the novel that the events can be fully reassembled and understood. This is deliberate, of course, as Morrison herself has pointed out:

> Whatever the risk of confronting the reader with what must be immediately incomprehensible [...] the risk of unsettling him or her, I determined to take it. Because the in-medias-res opening that I am so committed to is here excessively demanding. It is abrupt, and should appear so. No native informant here. The

reader is snatched, yanked, thrown into an environment completely foreign, and I want it as the first stroke of the shared experience that might be possible between the reader and the novel's population. Snatched just as the slaves were from one place to another, from any place to another, without preparation and without defence[1].

Morrison places her reader in the middle of the action without providing background information. She wants it to be a disorientating experience because she feels readers should share the characters' view of a world that is as incomprehensible to them. African people were snatched from their homeland and transported to an unfamiliar country, and while it is impossible to appreciate how traumatic this would have been, it is nevertheless apt that disorientation should play a part in the author's strategy in a novel about slavery. Though the characters are no longer slaves when the novel begins, their world is still unfathomable and frightening, struggling as they are to make sense of their past and find meaning for their lives in the present. By limiting our perspective to theirs Morrison forces us to dwell in the moment, to share their bewilderment and perhaps better appreciate their anxiety and pain.

The focus is on a single house, 124 Bluestone Road, and on the family who live there. Sethe—the principal character in the novel—is an ex-slave who worked on the ironically named Sweet Home plantation in Kentucky; Baby Suggs is her mother-in-law, whose freedom from Sweet Home was paid for by her son, Sethe's husband, Halle. Sethe and Halle were separated when they attempted to escape the planation eighteen years earlier, and Sethe hasn't seen him since. Sethe had four children with Halle: those that survive are two boys, Howard and Buglar, and a girl, Denver, the youngest child.

When the novel opens, Baby Suggs is dead, and the boys have left the house, scared off by a ghost that is haunting it. This is thought to be the spirit of Sethe's dead baby, Beloved, who died when she was two years old. Sethe was forced to have sex with an engraver to pay for the lettering on her daughter's gravestone: she intended to mark

---

1　Toni Morrison. 'Unspeakable Things Unspoken: The Afro-American Presence in American Literature.' See online resources.

it with the words 'Dearly Beloved,' but ten minutes of sex only paid for seven letters. Beloved would have been Sethe's third child and the number of their house on Bluestone Road, 124, is meant to represent her absence.

The ghost of Beloved is angry and spiteful, but Baby Suggs felt it would be pointless to move from 124 because, 'Not a house in the country ain't packed to its rafters with some dead Negro's grief. We lucky this ghost is a baby.'[5] This statement makes a link between the haunting of 124 and the general legacy of African American suffering, which Beloved is later seen to symbolise. It also marks an attitude to the supernatural that is somewhat different from that associated with contemporary Western society. Baby Suggs—indeed all the characters in the novel—accept the spiritual world as a simple fact of life.

Ghosts signify in different ways in literature but generally they imply that there are things cannot die. More specifically in *Beloved*, the notion of haunting is suggestive of the things that black people cannot forget or repress following their years of enslavement and mistreatment. Certainly the prospect of psychological or emotional reconstruction—which is a central requirement for the novel's protagonists and the community as a whole—seems unlikely with such an angry ghost around.

Also in this first chapter we learn that the act of remembering is an issue. All Baby Suggs can remember of her eight children is the fact that the first born liked the taste of burnt bread; Sethe suggests that this is because Baby Suggs forces herself *not* to remember. Inevitably memories are painful for ex-slaves, particularly for mothers. When a slave gave birth the child automatically became the property of the slave owner, and their lives would be subject to the will of that owner. Sethe also has trouble remembering: her memory of her son, Buglar, is fading, for instance, and she tries hard to forget certain aspects of her life on the plantation. Indeed, she feels as if she is being 'punished' for remembering when Paul D turns up at 124. He is a flesh and blood visitor from the past; a Sweet Home slave who'd been strongly attracted to Sethe when she was brought to the plantation as a young girl. The other male slaves, Paul F., Paul A., Sixo and

Halle, all wanted her too, and she was allowed to choose which one to marry, spending a year before deciding on Halle.

Sethe and Paul D have strong connection thanks to their shared history and mutual attraction. When he arrives at 124 Sethe tells him about her having been abused at Sweet Home by schoolteacher, the plantation manager, and his nephews: the latter beat her so badly that she still has scars shaped like a chokecherry tree on her back; even more humiliating for Sethe is the fact that the men stole her milk. Both of these things resonate powerfully throughout the book. The chokecherry tree—suggestive of the Biblical tree of knowledge and Adam and Eve's suffering—is a physical scar to parallel the psychological scars that Sethe carries. Ironically it is an aesthetically beautiful image, a contrast to the horror of the beating itself. Sethe's milk is a more complex symbol, representing the connection between mother and child, and the nurturing instinct that is central to our humanity. In essence it denotes the opposite of slavery: the later breaks down such connections, overriding natural bonds like those born of motherhood and love. Sethe feels that the act of taking her milk is the ultimate violation: amid all the cruelty and indignity she experienced as a slave, it is this dehumanising act that traumatises her most of all.

Paul D kisses Sethe's scars and cups her breasts; as he does so she feels she is 'relieved of their weight,' suggesting that Paul is the potential source of respite from the burdens she's endured. However there is also a sense in which he is laying claim to her, and as Paul D holds Sethe the house begins to shake with the ghost's disapproval; he grabs the legs of a table that comes flying towards him and begins beating the room, ordering the spirit to leave. Eventually the house falls still and it looks as if the spirit has been banished. The chapter does not end on a positive note however: while Sethe and Paul D climb the stairs to make love, Denver is left alone. She has no friends, and the family members she cared for are gone: because her brothers have left home and Baby Suggs is dead, the only companion she had was the ghost that Paul D has banished, and the chapter closes hinting at her misery and resentment.

4.2 Chapters Two and Three

Sethe and Paul D have sex but it is over quickly and is unsatisfactory. After the initial attraction, Paul D sees Sethe's disfigured body in a less positive way. In the scene that follows the two of them pursue their own thoughts. Once more we are presented with flashbacks to their life at Sweet Home, including details of Sethe and Halle's marriage. Sethe told the plantation owner, Mrs Garner that she would like a wedding dress but the latter only laughs. Marriages between slaves were not considered valid, and had no real meaning: the marriage contract implies a degree of self-ownership that is incompatible with slavery. Sethe makes her own wedding dress in secret, however, such is her desire to give their union some significance. We also learn of Sixo's relationship with a slave girl known as the Thirty Mile Woman. She is so called because Sixo would walk a nocturnal trip of thirty four miles to meet her, again suggesting something about the lengths the slaves would go in order to facilitate companionship, or a limited sense of self-determination. Sixo tries his best to maintain a degree of autonomy in his world, going out 'night-creeping' after work, sacrificing precious hours of rest for a fleeting experience of freedom. He would also dance among the trees at night, 'to keep his bloodlines open' [25]. It is not entirely clear what this means, but it is worth noting that there is an interesting emphasis on fluidity throughout the novel: the notion of flow both within and between individuals seems to be important. It reminds us, for instance, of the reference to Sethe's breast milk in chapter one, and the natural flow between mother and infant that is undermined by schoolteacher's nephews. As we've seen, this human connection is at odds with slavery: it is a flow that slavery stymies. Also, at the outset of the book the flow between the past and the present seems to be impeded: people find it difficult to remember the painful past, but we get the impression that this is important. In this sense again, then, flow needs to be established, or re-established. For Sixo, keeping things flowing—in his case the 'bloodlines'—is an essential thing, and this notion complements one of the novel's themes.

   To some extent chapter two is about the birth of relationships, and eventually Sethe and Paul D become more comfortable with one another, suggesting the possibility of an enduring union, and perhaps a chance of happiness for both of them.

In chapter three it is clear that Denver is not comfortable having Paul D around and she resents that the ghost departed with his arrival. She once had a vision of her mother praying with a figure at her side which took the form of a white dress with its arm around Sethe; it seemed portentous and she associates it with the ghost of the baby, concluding that it had 'plans,' though 'Whatever [those plans] might have been, Paul D messed them up for good' [37].

Denver is incredibly lonely and very secretive, seeking solitude in the woods in a space made by boxwood bushes. Here, 'closed off from the hurt of the hurt of the world,' [28] she finds solace in her imagination. Where Sethe and Paul D find it difficult to confront the past, Denver obsessively seeks details about her history. The chapter relates some of the things Sethe has told her about her past, specifically how she was born with the help of the young white girl, Amy–Denver. Sethe had fled Sweet Home while pregnant, damaging her feet in the process. Amy, who was on her way to Boston, massages them, and when Sethe cries in relief and agony Amy says: "Anything dead coming back to life hurts." [35] These words become significant as the novel develops—they clearly relate to the forthcoming reincarnation of Beloved, an apparent example of the past coming back to life.

Rememory

Sethe's own view of the past is revealed in this chapter too, specifically her opinion it never goes away:

> If a house burns down, it's gone, but the place—the picture of it—stays, and not just in my rememory, but out there, in the world. What I remember is a picture floating around there outside my head. I mean, even if I don't think about it, even if I die, the picture of what I did, or knew, or saw is still out there [36]

Sethe resists the traditional notion of history as something that is linear, and over as soon as it's happened. Her view has similarities with certain African belief systems which deem the past to be part of the present, informing the lives of the living; and that includes the pain and horror of what has happened to oneself and others. The term 'rememory' refers to encounters with memories, then, and importantly Sethe is not referring merely to psychological encounters, but material ones, 'out there' in the world. One of the ways in which 'rememory' differs from remembering is that it has an existence independent of the individual: memories are things for Sethe, and they extend beyond her personal consciousness. This in turn implies that memories can be shared: they have a presence in the world that can impact on anyone who encounters them. It is a different way of conceiving of events and time that necessitates adjusting one's frame of reference; it is unsettling for Denver who worries about running into a past that is 'still waiting for her,' [42] and she becomes reluctant to leave 124 as a result. It suggests that Sethe is frightened of her memories too, and that there are aspects of the past from which she wants to shield her daughter, and herself. At the same time, of course, this view of the past implies that it's all the more important to seek ways of being reconciled with it. If it is inescapable, as Sethe seems to think, then sooner or later it will need to be confronted. The notion of rememory, with its prefix 're' underscores the inevitability of memories (re)surfacing, and of the individual being forced to (re)visit the past. Indeed there is a sense in which 'rememory' becomes part of the novel's strategy for telling Sethe's story: as will be seen the central event of infanticide is revisited repeatedly, despite Sethe's attempts to keep it from her conscious mind. Later in the novel Sethe's view of the past will have a bearing on how she interprets Beloved when she appears at 124: her concept of rememory legitimises perpetual material presence and so makes the physical re-emergence of her daughter completely plausible to her.

So Sethe conceives of the past as something that never goes away, and the word 'rememory,' working as both a verb and a noun, is used as a replacement for 'remember' and 'memory' because it is more organic in the way it links the individual to the past; it is also inclusive, suggestive of the past as eternally present.

At the end of chapter three Sethe tells Paul D that schoolteacher sought her out after she escaped Sweet Home but that she went to jail rather than go back to the plantation. She does not elaborate, and Paul D does not press the issue, partly because he has his own painful memories of incarceration, working on a chain gang in Alfred, Georgia. But a more positive future still seems to be a possibility at this stage, and Sethe in particular is hopeful: the idea of a future with Paul D 'was beginning to stroke her mind' [42].

4.3 Chapters Four, Five and Six

Chapter Four begins with an argument between Paul D and Sethe. Denver causes this by voicing her suspicion of Paul D, asking him how long he plans to stay at 124. Paul wonders if Denver is airing a question that is also on Sethe's mind, but she denies this. More importantly he wonders if Sethe isn't too protective of Denver; her desire to shield her daughter is based on love and Paul feels that it is risky for ex-slaves to love, particularly when it comes to their children. Slaves have a history of having things taken away from them and too much emotional investment creates too much trauma when this happens. As the argument develops we learn that Sethe is reluctant to explore her feelings and her inner life: 'I don't go inside' she tells him [46]. Paul D offers his support, pledging to help her 'Go as far inside' as she needs to, and promising to hold on to Sethe's ankles to prevent her from being consumed by the darkness within. Again this is a reference to the difficulty Sethe has confronting the past and her memories: there are some thoughts that she struggles to keep out of her conscious mind. Paul D's pledge to assist her introduces the notion that such traumas should be addressed with the help of others. Just as Amy helped Sethe cope when she was in most need—messaging her back to life—so it looks as if Paul D might help facilitate another recovery for Sethe; it suggests that human beings are at their strongest when working together. Sethe's cautious optimism about her future is reinforced in chapter four, then, and it ends with Paul D, Sethe and Denver taking a trip to a local carnival: even Denver seems to enjoy herself here, and Sethe smiles readily, imagining that their shadows are holding hands.

When they return home from the carnival they encounter a young woman near to 124 who appears to have emerged from the water fully dressed. When Sethe sees her she is overcome by an urge to urinate, and when she voids her bladder it is reminiscent of a woman's waters breaking at childbirth. The girl has remarkably smooth skin, a profound thirst, and her name is Beloved. She sleeps on and off for four days, tended by Denver who develops a deep affection for her, becoming unnaturally possessive in the process. Their dog, Here Boy, disappears on Beloved's arrival and Denver seems to know instinctively that he won't be back. The dog had been injured during the time when 124 was haunted, and his disappearance suggests a connection between Beloved and the recently departed ghost. Also Beloved's appearance seems to reopen the rift between Denver and Paul D: when the latter looks to her to corroborate his observation that Beloved had lifted a chair and thus seems stronger than she claims to be, Denver refuses. For his part Paul D is extremely unsettled by Beloved: he is sickened by her obsession with sweet things, and although he respects her reluctance to talk about her past, knowing how traumatic this can be for black people, he is markedly suspicious of her.

In the following chapter we see Beloved become progressively devoted to Sethe, and she likes to hear her tell stories about her life. This is hard for Sethe because 'Everything in it was painful or lost' [58], but Beloved has a way bringing the past back into the conscious mind. For instance, she seems to have knowledge of earrings that Sethe once owned, and as Sethe tells her about them she finds herself enjoying the experience, remembering things that she'd formerly forgotten, or didn't even know she knew. She recalls a conversation she had with her mother and the seemingly repressed fact that her mother had been hanged. She also recalls an exchange with a woman called Nan who'd travelled to America on the same slave ship as her mother. The two were raped many times by the crew, and Sethe's mother threw away the resulting offspring; the only child she kept was Sethe, the product of a union with a black man who she felt affection for and who 'she put her arms around' during sex; Sethe is named after this man. The conversation between Sethe and Nan had been conducted in an African language that Sethe no longer under-stands, but the tale itself re-emerges with clarity, surprising Sethe. We begin to see that Beloved is able stimulate recollections, and this is one of the important functions she serves: she becomes a catalyst for lost or repressed memories. This is not restricted to Sethe's per-sonal history either: the reference to her memory of the lost language of Africa reminds us of all those who were forcibly taken from their country and robbed, not only of freedom, but of their history, culture and identity; it suggests a link between Sethe's suffering and the gen-eral trauma of the enslaved.

Beloved appears to be able to make the past come alive again, then, and it seems as if she herself is a literal example of the past returning. The characters start to associate Beloved with the child who haunted 124, and these associations are reinforced by her childlike behaviour: her constant napping, her craving for sweet things, her unsteadiness on her feet and in her speech and, not least, her apparent inability to detach herself from her newfound mother, Sethe.

4.4 Chapters Seven and Eight

Paul D's anxieties about Beloved increase in chapter seven, and he is annoyed that she is inhibiting his relationship with Sethe; he also becomes suspicious of her unwillingness to discuss her background, and wary of her strange, 'shining' sexuality. When he tries to quiz Beloved about her past he gets into an argument with Sethe who feels he is being too harsh with her. It is clear that the young woman is coming between them and this compounds our increasing sense of her as a potentially dark force. Following the argument, Paul tells Sethe that Halle witnessed the incident when schoolteacher's neph-ews stole her milk. It apparently drove him insane, for Paul later saw him sitting by a churn with butter smeared all over his face; the sight of his wife being violated in this way seemingly 'broke him like a twig' [68]. At the time Paul couldn't converse with Halle because he himself was wearing an iron bit between his teeth as a punish-ment. Paul recalls feeling lower than the roosters and chickens on the plantation because of this: they appeared to be free in ways that he was not. He recalls specifically a rooster called Mister, who seemed to have an identity that he lacked: 'Even if you cooked him you'd be cooking a rooster called Mister'[72]; by contrast Paul D is not a 'Mister,' having been unmanned by schoolteacher. The experience was profoundly dehumanising for Paul, and he is still struggling to come to terms with it. Being treated like an animal was an affront to his masculinity and the shame of it has crippled his self-respect. The memory is so traumatic that Paul is surprised he told Sethe about it, and he is not sure where the impulse came from. The implication is that this new willingness to explore the past has to do with Beloved; she seems to inspire or facilitate it. However, while there is much more that Paul could tell Sethe about his slave experiences, he cannot yet manage to fully share. Like Sethe, he still finds his memories too painful and shaming to confront. This is expressed figuratively in the form of the tobacco tin in which he feels his secrets are stored, 'buried in his chest where a red heart used to be. Its lid rusted shut' [72–73].

The eighth chapter begins with Denver and Beloved dancing, and Denver asking her questions about her experiences before she appeared in their lives. Beloved tells her of a hot dark place where it was so overcrowded she couldn't move; there were people piled upon people, some of whom were dead. This could be a reference to a Middle Passage experience, suggestive of the kind of slave-ship crossing that black people endured when they were transported from Africa. Here, and again later in the novel, there is a suggestion that Beloved may either have experienced this herself, or that she may be in touch with the collective unconscious of African Americans, and a shared memory of such a crossing. When Denver asks why she came to 124 Beloved says that it was to see Sethe because 'she left me behind. By myself' [75]. This implies again that she is Denver's sister reborn, and when Denver pleads with her not to reveal this to Sethe Beloved becomes angry, warning Denver never to tell her what to do. Denver placates Beloved and tells her the story that Sethe has often related about the circumstances of her birth. The story is told in detail, and this is the first time Denver has been able to imagine it in such richness and complexity: we are told that 'she was seeing it now and feeling it—through Beloved. Feeling how it must have felt for her mother' [78]. Again it appears that Beloved becomes a catalyst for stories of the past, in this instance allowing Denver to unpack the tale of her birth in a way that allows her to appreciate it more fully. Denver's tale reveals how she owes her survival to an act of kindness from a white girl, and that the actual birth itself was success against the odds because Sethe and Amy were able to work together. We are told that there were no paterollers (people who rounded up runaway slaves) or preachers to encroach on the natural female business of childbirth, and as a consequence nature took its course. Again this seems to stress the possibility that problems can be overcome by working together, anticipating the ending of the novel when Beloved is finally exorcised by a community of women acting in unison.

4.5 Chapters Nine, Ten and Eleven

In chapter nine we learn more about Baby Suggs and her status in the community as a lay preacher. Before she died she would offer inspirational words in the 'Clearing,' encouraging the people to laugh and cry with abandon, and most importantly to love their bodies. Baby Suggs feels that black people should love their bodies because white people despise them. Slavery maintained that their bodies were owned by someone other than themselves and so learning to love one's body is an act of reclamation. For Baby Suggs loving the body—the material fact of it—is an exercise in self-ownership, and an essential part of rediscovering oneself and asserting one's status as a human being. This notion is at odds with Paul D's inclination to keep his feelings in a tin. In his view it is reckless to love anything too much, but Baby Suggs's words imply that this means cutting oneself off from the possibility of redemption or significant connection with others; it is vital to embrace love rather than to fear it. Baby Suggs has a spiritual dimension and the ability to convey a message that the community can relate to, this is why they use the word 'holy' after her name.

Sethe reminisces about Baby Suggs and we learn how she found her way to her house after Amy had helped deliver Denver. She was aided by Stamp Paid and Ella, both of whom were involved with the Underground Railroad. This was a network of secret routes through which escaped slaves could find their way to free states. During the years of slavery these routes ran between safe houses—termed stations or depots—kept by people called stationmasters. The slaves were known as passengers and their journey between safe spaces was facilitated by conductors. It is Ella who gets Sethe to 124, and Baby Suggs welcomes her, reuniting her with the children she sent on ahead: her two boys and 'the crawling-already girl' who becomes known as Beloved. Initially it appeared that Sethe's escape had been successful, and Sethe began to heal, listening to Baby Suggs speaking in the Clearing and feeling part of the community.

Sethe decides to take Denver and Beloved to the Clearing where Baby Suggs used to preach. While there she feels what at first seem like the fingers of Baby Suggs's spirit massaging her neck, although suddenly the pressure increases and she has the impression of being strangled. Afterwards Beloved strokes and kisses the bruises, but while this is soothing at first, it starts to become discomfiting for Sethe who asks her stop. Later Denver accuses Beloved of causing Sethe to choke but she denies it, leaving Denver to puzzle over the incident, and once more reminisce about her own early life. We learn that she had once attended the school run by Lady Jones who'd taught her to spell and count. She'd enjoyed it for a year until a fellow pupil, Nelson Lord, said 'Didn't your mother get locked away for murder? Wasn't you in there with her when she went'; Denver, 'went deaf rather than hear the answer' [104/5]. Here we see one of the reasons for Denver's isolation and lack of emotional development: she has become cut off from the world outside 124 and intimated by the idea of engaging with it. At the same time she craves companionship, and envies those who have it, even feeling jealous of the relationships between Sethe's fellow slaves on the plantation.

In this chapter we also learn about the lesson Baby Suggs feels she has learned from life: on the afternoon before she died she told Sethe and Denver that 'there was no bad luck in the world but white people. "They don't know when to stop," she said' [104]. Baby Suggs has been irrevocably affected by white people because there were apparently no limits to the lengths they would go to enforce slavery; people who can justify such cruelty can presumably rationalise anything. Of course this view is at odds with the compassion shown by Amy when she helped Sethe in an act that put her own safely at risk.

We get a sense of how far whites can go in their abuse of black people when we learn of Paul D's ordeal in prison in Alfred. He'd been sent there for trying to kill Brandywine, the man to whom he'd been sold by schoolteacher. Here he was kept in a wooden box in a ditch alongside forty five other men. They were woken with rifle shots, beaten, and forced to perform oral sex on the guards. They would work chained together in the daytime, and find respite only in singing and dreaming of revenge on those persecuting them, and on 'Life for leading them on' [109]. Paul and the rest of the chain gang are able to escape after a severe rainstorm destroys the trench. They find their way to a camp of Cherokee who feed them and help free them from their chains. This is another indication of the importance of working together; it is only because the prisoners act as a group that they are able to escape, and it is only with the assistance of the Cherokee—another group oppressed by white people—that they are able to survive. They point the way to freedom for Paul, who finally ends up with a 'weaver lady' in Delaware with whom he stays for eighteen months, she passing him off as her nephew from Syracuse. Here, then, we learn more about the extent of Paul D's suffering and the terrible memories stored in 'the tobacco tin lodged in his chest;' we can understand why 'By the time he got to 124 nothing in this world could pry it open' [113].

Almost imperceptibly Paul finds himself moving out of 124, and the implication is that Beloved is behind this. Initially he'd been sleeping with Sethe but he begins sleeping elsewhere for reasons that aren't clear to him; he tries different rooms in the house feeling dissatisfied with each in turn, until eventually moving to the cold house which was 'separated from the main part of 124' [116]. It seems as if Paul had good reason to be wary of Beloved's 'shining' sexuality because she begins to visit him here, asking him to put his fingers in her vagina. To begin with he resists, but eventually complies and the encounter has a marked effect on him, figuratively freeing up the rusted lid on his tobacco tin. Once again it seems as if Beloved has the power to facilitate engagement with painful memories. The rusted-shut tin had been lodged in his heart, but Paul begins chanting the phrase, 'Red heart. Red Heart. Red heart' over and over, implying that the act has put Paul back in touch with something fundamental to his humanity; it suggests that his metaphorical heart has been set beating again, a formally retarded flow is in motion again.

4.6 Chapters Twelve, Thirteen and Fourteen

Denver's obsession with Beloved is becoming more intense: she covets her attention, and when Beloved looks at her she experiences a feeling of wholeness. Denver has the impression that Beloved needs something, although it isn't clear what. She has convinced herself that Beloved is a reincarnation of the baby who had previously haunted the house, but she keeps this to herself. Sethe no longer seems to think this, however, and begins to wonder whether or not she is an escaped sex slave. There is a precedent for this among the people Sethe knows: Ella, the woman who helped Stamp Paid assist runaway slaves, was abused in such a way; she was imprisoned by a father and son for their sexual pleasure. The fact the she no longer thinks in terms of Beloved being her murdered daughter—even though it seems obvious to Denver—implies that Sethe still struggles to deal with the incident, and so represses that horrific memory.

Beloved's behaviour is markedly childlike: she craves Sethe's attention in an extremely needy way, reminiscent of a spoilt toddler. In Sethe's absence she gravitates towards Denver who relishes this attention and works carefully to cultivate it. She tries to entertain her with stories about her life and the few people she has met like Lady Jones and a boy with the nickel birthmark who was her fellow pupil, and of course her family: Sethe, Baby Suggs, and the absent Howard and Buglar. She wants to know more about Beloved but feels she will scare her off with her questioning; she is desperate to keep her close, so much so that when Beloved sleeps she leans over and sniffs her sugary breath. Before Beloved's arrival Denver was lonely and her apparently reincarnated sister represents an alternative to that former life of solitude; she comes to see Beloved as essential to her life, and it is almost as if Denver has no identity without her: Beloved's gaze seems to confirm her sense of self. At one point they are in the cold house and Denver loses sight of Beloved and panics thinking she has gone from her life. When she finds her, Beloved acts strangely, telling Denver that 'This is the place I am,' before curling up on the floor, rocking and softly moaning. Beloved mentions a face—'Her face'—and when Denver asks her who she is referring to she replies, 'It's me' [124]. This is suggestive of the references Beloved makes to the 'other place' elsewhere in the novel—this is the place where she is aware of being before her arrival at 124. It is never really clear what this is: it could be a reference to her mother's womb; it could be a reference to her experience of travelling on a slave ship—the Middle Passage—or it could be a reference to her incarceration as a sex slave. Obviously if we are meant to see Beloved as a reincarnation of Sethe's murdered child, then it could also refer to her experiences prior to being reborn: the place she occupied before her rebirth. When Beloved refers to the 'the place where I am' she could be indicating the woodshed where she was murdered, obviously giving more weight to the notion that she is Sethe's daughter reborn.

In chapter thirteen we find that Paul D's desire for Beloved makes him feel like a slave again; he is reminded of how schoolteacher would dehumanise black people, and render them impotent: 'bulls without horns; gelded workhorses' [125]. Paul had always maintained hope and strength from his knowledge that schoolteacher was wrong in his views, but now Beloved had once more robbed him of his autonomy, and he feels like a rag doll 'picked up and put back down anywhere anytime by a girl young enough to be his daughter' [126]. Unmanned once more, Paul D decides that a way of breaking free of Beloved might be to tell Sethe about his liaisons with her. Ultimately he cannot summon the courage to do this, but he finds himself asking Sethe if she will consider having his child. Sethe refuses but invites Paul D back into her bed, infuriating Beloved, but freeing Paul from her weird influence. In the next chapter Beloved asks Denver if she can make Paul D go away and during the conversation pulls one of her own teeth out. As Beloved feels that she's losing her influence over Sethe, she fears she is falling apart: it is as if she needs to sustain her relationship with Sethe in order to be whole.

4.7 Chapter Fifteen

In this chapter we learn more about Baby Suggs and her history as a slave at Sweet Home. She was treated comparatively well there because no one beat her, and her owners Mr and Mrs Garner were good natured and kind. However, we get a sense of how slavery has robbed her of her identity. The Garner's call her Jenny because the name Jenny Whitlow was on the bill of sale when she was purchased, so in essence she was nameless. Indeed she has been denied all the things that constitute identity: not just her name but her family, most notably her children, seven of whom were taken away before she could become a mother to them or learn what course their lives took. Family provides a context for one's sense of self, of course, and without this knowledge and history of human engagement Baby Suggs feels hollow. Despite not knowing whether the majority of her children are alive or dead, she still knows more about them than she knows about herself. We are told that she 'never had the map to discover what she was like,' because she has been denied the usual narrative of family and friends:

> 'Could she sing? (Was it nice to hear when she did?) Was she pretty? Was she a good friend? Could she have been a loving mother? A faithful wife? Have I got a sister and does she favour me? If my mother knew me would she like me?'[140]

The things that slavery denies are the things that combine to make a person; without them Baby Suggs feels that her so-called self is 'no self.'

The one child that Baby Suggs *was* allowed to keep, Halle, paid for her freedom, and when that day came Mr Garner drove her to 124 Bluestone Road. This is a house owned by a brother and sister called the Bodwins who allow her to stay in return for work. Garner advises her to keep the name Jenny now that she is free, but Baby Suggs refuses, preferring her husband's name, Suggs, together with the name he always called her: Baby. This is an indication of her desire to take control of her identity in her new free life. Her ability to choose a name is a reflection of her new found liberty, and of her ability to defy her previous owner's counsel.

Also in this chapter we're told about Sethe's initial arrival at Bluestone Road. To celebrate this Baby Suggs made pies using beautiful berries picked by Stamp Paid, and this developed into a huge feast for the community. However, the townsfolk grew resentful and came to see the repast as an indication of pride and excess. Their resentment took the edge off Sethe's arrival, and Baby Suggs began to sense a bad omen behind this resentment which foreshadows the arrival of schoolteacher in the next chapter. As it turns out some of the community are aware that schoolteacher is coming but they fail to warn Sethe. This reminds us that black people can be as petty and cruel as white people, and it implies that it is wrong to think of morality in terms of race.

4.8 Chapters Sixteen and Seventeen

Sethe has been free for twenty eight days when schoolteacher arrives to claim her. It is significant that this is the duration of the female menstrual cycle because it links freedom to the body, and the body's natural rhythms and phases: a contrast to the unnatural impositions of slavery. It reflects Sethe's status as a woman and a human being, something that schoolteacher refuses to acknowledge. It is also suggestive of motherhood and the body's potential to create a future outside slavery.

Schoolteacher arrives with three others—his nephew, a slave catcher, and the sheriff—and their arrival alludes to the four horsemen of the Apocalypse: famine, plague, war, and death. Just as the biblical horseman mark the coming of humanity's destruction in The Book of Revelations, so here they mark the end of Sethe's peaceful sojourn at 124. On their arrival Sethe kills Beloved with a saw and is about to dash Denver's head against the wall but Stamp Paid manages to stop her. Howard and Buglar are found bleeding on the floor, but survive after being tended by Baby Suggs. The chapter is narrated mainly from schoolteacher's point of view and offers an insight into his racist assumptions about black people. He assumes that Sethe has become ungovernable because she has been overbeaten, and he compares her 'education' to the training of an animal, using the pronoun 'it' to refer to his subject. He regrets this because Sethe was a good worker who still had 'at least ten breeding years left' [149]. The episode confirms his opinion that black people need looking after if they are not to revert to the primitive behavior he feels characterizes their race. When it becomes clear to schoolteacher that his property is damaged beyond repair he leaves.

Baby Suggs takes the dead child from Sethe and gives her Denver to nurse, but Baby is furious when Sethe allows Denver to feed from her nipple without first washing away Beloved's blood: she tries to retake Denver but Sethe is too strong and Denver takes her milk along with her dead sister's blood. The chapter closes with the sheriff taking Sethe and Denver away as a throng of people look on in stunned silence.

In the following chapter Stamp Paid shows Paul D a newspaper clipping that reports the incident and subsequent trial. Paul finds it hard to believe that it relates to Sethe because the sketch accompanying the clipping fails to capture her. Paul cannot read so Stamp reads the article for him, but omits much of what he saw with his own eyes. Stamp relates some of this to the reader, however, and his memory of Sethe's hawk-like flight to the empty woodshed with her children offers another perspective on the incident. Paul D still refuses to believe it could be Sethe, and his conviction almost makes Stamp doubt what he'd seen with his own eyes. Paul cannot reconcile the horror of that incident with the woman he knows because he has seen her capacity to love and care for others, not just her own offspring but him too, and his response to the bald facts reminds us that we should always be suspicious of them. Stories involving human beings are invariably more complex than can be adequately represented in a newspaper article, or indeed any narrative.

4.9 Chapter Eighteen

When Paul D seeks more details from Sethe about what Stamp told him she begins walking round the room in circles, making him dizzy. She tells him about her feelings when she escaped Sweet Home and how it changed her relationship with her children. There is a sense in which her freedom gave her the capacity to love them properly: Paul can identify with this because for him too freedom meant being able to love without asking permission. As Sethe continues to circle she begins to drift away from the issue, but the reader sees her thoughts and memories of the moment schoolteacher came for her:

> She was squatting in the garden and when she saw them coming and recognized schoolteacher's hat, she heard wings. Little hummingbirds stuck their needle beaks right through her headcloth into her hair and beat their wings. And if she thought anything, it was No, No. Nono. Nonono. Simple. She just flew. Collected every bit of life she had made, all the parts of her that were precious and fine and beautiful, and carried, pushed, dragged them though the veil, out, away, over there where no one could hurt them. Over there. Outside this place, where they would be safe. And the hummingbird wings beat on [163].

Sethe remembers an emphatic refusal to relinquish her children, suggested by the repetition of 'No'. The images of flying remind us of her escape from Sweet Home and the fleeting freedom she has enjoyed; now she is forced to fly again. The image of the birds' needle beaks conveys her panic, and this image will return again later in the story. She seems only to have her children's safety on her mind, together with vague notions of a place where they might avoid schoolteacher and his potential to hurt them. She sees them as part of herself, and perhaps her sense of ownership legitimizes her actions: because she can't see a distinction between her flesh and theirs her assault is more akin to self-harm than murder; perhaps it could even be construed as self-defence? But what strikes the reader most of all is how her actions appear to have been instinctive; again this is reinforced to some extent by the bird imagery and the verb to fly: she is compelled to act by something innate which precludes considered moral reflection.

Paul D does not understand how Sethe could have harmed her children, and he begins to see her differently, viewing her actions almost as the effect of self-absorption, or narcissism: 'This here new Sethe didn't know where the world stopped and she began' [164]; for him her willingness to see her children as extensions of herself is contemptible. 'Your love is too thick' he says, suggesting how it encompasses her children without respect for boundaries, transcending even their right to life. He accuses Sethe of behaving like an animal by saying 'You got two feet, Sethe, not four,' [165]. This is a profound insult for Sethe given her history of being treated like an animal at Sweet Home; as an ex-slave Paul D knows all too well how hurtful and offensive this will be, and he leaves without saying goodbye.

Part Two

4.10 Chapter Nineteen

Stamp Paid feels guilty about having shown Paul D the newspaper article and so he decides to pay a visit to 124: he feels he has a duty to offer his services out of respect for Baby Suggs, a woman he knew well and admired. Stamp has a history of helping the community and is esteemed by all, so he does not usually knock before entering black people's homes. However he feels reluctant to enter 124 but is not sure why; he returns to the house several times before summoning-up the courage to knock. When he does actually knock no one answers; he looks through the window of the house and is unsettled by the sight of Beloved whose presence he cannot account for.

With Paul D gone, Sethe, Denver and Beloved are living alone in 124. Sethe is now convinced that Beloved is indeed her daughter returned from the dead, her mind having been made up on hearing her hum a song that Sethe sang solely to her children. Deciding that the focus of her life should be her daughters, Sethe has turned her back on the world because she does not feel that there is anything worth having beyond 124: 'The world is this room,' she says, 'This here's all there is and all there needs to be' [183].

Sethe begins stealing food from the restaurant where she works, and goes into psychological decline, losing touch with what is appropriate. Her thieving brings to mind an incident at Sweet Home involving Sixo, and she begins to reminisce about the time he stole a piece of meat and, when accused of stealing by schoolteacher, attempted to justify his actions with a clever argument. Sixo claimed that he would be able to work harder after eating the meat, ultimately benefiting Sweet Home and schoolteacher. Though schoolteacher appreciates the logic of this argument he beat Sixo anyway in order to stress that 'definitions belong to the definers—not to the defined' [190]. This makes an important point about the nature of power and the influence powerful people have over what counts as truth. For instance, schoolteacher's definition of black people as inferior is indicative of the white elite who wished to sustain and justify slavery: their definition of blacks as subhuman is imposed on the slaves not because it is valid, of course, but because those whose interests are served by that notion occupy the position of authority; power rather than truth creates the definition.

Formerly life at Sweet Home had been relatively good for the slaves: the owners Mr and Mrs Garner were generally kind to them. However when Garner dies and his wife is taken ill, schoolteacher is asked to manage the plantation; his treatment of the slaves is much harsher, and he has a completely different attitude to their status in life: for him black people are essentially sub-human. Sethe recalls an episode when she overheard schoolteacher teaching his nephews about black people: one of them uses her as an example as schoolteacher instructs him to separate her human characteristics from her animal characteristics, and list them side by side. Schoolteacher once used a 'measuring string' to measure Sethe, and she now sees that he was studying her as an object of scientific enquiry. Schoolteacher represents a particular character type and way of thinking: he is the kind of nineteenth century rationalist who defended slavery on scientific grounds, thinking it is possible to categorize human and animal traits empirically and distinguish whites from blacks in this way. When Sethe hears schoolteacher talking about her as an animal she feels 'Like somebody was sticking fine needles in my scalp,' which brings to mind the 'needle beaks' of the hummingbirds she feels sticking 'through her headcloth' when later he tries to recapture her. Again it underscores her sense of terror, this time at the realisation that she is perceived as little more than a beast by some white people. Though *Beloved* as a novel insists on moral complexity, it is hard to see schoolteacher as anything other than unequivocally wicked. His cruelty is further revealed in this chapter when he insists that Halle does extra work for free at Sweet Home. Halle had been working off the plantation to buy his mother's freedom, but schoolteacher makes him redirect this extra work to Sweet Home, and refuses to pay extra for it. This effectively traps his family forever: without the possibility of earning additional money there is no way of facilitating their freedom. Such brutality becomes the catalyst for a plan to escape using the Underground Railroad. Sethe sends her children on ahead and eventually escapes herself, but the plan is disastrous for Sixo and Paul A, both of whom are killed during the attempt, and for Paul D who is caught and forced to wear a huge iron collar as a punishment.

While schoolteacher appears the embodiment of evil compared to the comparatively benign Mr Garner, Halle refuses to make a distinction between the two. When Sethe points out that the Garners are gentle and polite compared to schoolteacher, he tells her, 'What they say is the same. Loud or soft' [195]. He reminds her that, though they allowed him to buy Baby Suggs' freedom, this was hardly a charitable act because it was unlikely she would have been any use to them as an old lady anyway. For Halle a slave-owner is a slave-owner regardless of their personality: injustice and exploitation are inherent in the institution itself and cannot be mitigated by any positive traits those who endorse it might possess. This is an important point because the myth of the benign plantation owner is one that featured in the American consciousness throughout the history of slavery, and was often invoked in order to justify it. It implied a system of paternalism where slaves were looked after by kindly owners in return for their labour, inferring that slavery could be a reciprocal arrangement that was actually good for black people. Not only was it possible for slave owners to appease their own consciences in this way, it also gave a false impression of slavery that impeded social reform.

In this chapter we learn that Stamp Paid is so named because he once spared the life of a man who had sex with his wife. It was his master's son and his wife wouldn't allow him to take revenge for fear it would be suicidal. The name Stamp Paid refers to his feeling that, having not killed him, he now owes nothing to anyone. It suggests also that Stamp felt he had a moral right to exact revenge on the white man, and his restraint is evidence of his strength of character.

Stamp is angry when his friend Ella tells him that Paul D has been sleeping in the church basement; he spent much of his own life helping black people and feels the black community has a responsibility to provide mutual support. Through him we also learn more about the depression that Baby Suggs experienced following the murder at 124. She stopped her orations at the Clearing despite Stamp's attempts to persuade her to continue; instead she took to her bed and focused on thinking about colours on the grounds that they 'don't hurt nobody' [179]. It is only now, years after her death that Stamp begins to understand her point of view; she felt that her preaching didn't count because it couldn't keep the white people out of her yard when they came for Sethe. She was exhausted by the futility of her endeavours in the face of white power; indeed, at the end of her life she blames white people for all the trouble in the world. This theme is continued at the end of the chapter where we are given an insight into Stamp's views about white people and their attitude to African Americans:

> White people believed that whatever the manners, under every dark skin was a jungle. Swift unnavigable waters, swinging screaming baboons, sleeping snakes, red gums ready for their sweet white blood. In a way, he thought, they were right. The more coloredpeople spent their strength trying to convince them how gentle they were, how clever and loving, how human [...] the deeper and more tangled the jungle grew inside [...] But it wasn't the jungle blacks brought with them to this place [...] It was the jungle whitefolks planted in them. And it grew. It spread [...] until it invaded the whites who had made it [...] Made them bloody, silly, worse than even they wanted to be, so scared were they of the jungle they had made. The screaming baboon lived under their own white skin; the red gums were their own [198–199].

White people assume that black people are savages regardless of how they may appear on the surface. Any so-called civilized characteristics they exhibit are seen as a veneer; in fact, the more civilized they appear the greater the intensity of the assumed savagery. This alleged savagery has nothing to do with black people or their history: it is created by white people (the 'jungle they had made […] lived under their own white skin.') Here Stamp identifies the problems created when black people are constructed as 'other': whites assume that blacks are different and therefore dangerous, and they begin to define themselves in opposition to that assumed difference; black and white become reductive and antithetical terms, and fear, prejudice and hatred are the inevitable consequence. As an older man Stamp shares some of Baby Suggs's sense of futility in the face of white people's cruelty. Nothing seems to change: almost a decade after slavery has been abolished blacks are still suffering at the hands of whites, with lynchings, beatings, rapes, and theft a constant part of life. We are told that Stamp once happened upon a red ribbon with a piece of human hair attached—clearly from a girl who'd been scalped—and for him this has become symbolic of humanity's capacity for evil.

Outside 124 Stamp hears voices: we are told that the house is 'loud,' but the words he hears are almost incoherent except for the repetition of 'mine'. The narrator suggests that the voices are the 'unspoken' and 'unspeakable' thoughts of the women of 124. Stamp links the voices to his notion of the 'whitefolks' jungle' which perhaps suggests that they are the consequence of the injustice perpetrated on blacks because of this fear of the 'other'. If we are meant to see them as the ghost voices of maltreated black people, this marks a symbolic link between Beloved and black people's general history of suffering.

4.11 Chapters Twenty to Twenty Three

These four key chapters are presented as stream of consciousness narrative allowing us inside the minds of the characters and the flow of their thinking. They convey the 'unspeakable' thoughts that Stamp perceived but couldn't understand in the previous chapter. The first is told from Sethe's perspective and the opening line, 'Beloved, she my daughter. She mine,' reiterates her assumptions about Beloved, and links her statement of ownership to the voices Stamp Paid heard, and the one word he could understand: 'mine' [200]. References to Sethe's childhood, to Baby Suggs, Mrs Garner, Halle, and her mistreatment at Sweet Home come in a rush of unshaped images and allusions, and are linked ultimately to the return of her murdered daughter. We get some insight into her feelings about having murdered Beloved, which she sees as an act of love. Sethe thinks her own mother abandoned her when she was a baby, and she looks to distinguish her own actions from this desertion; she doesn't think that taking her daughter's life was abandonment; rather she was trying to save her by transporting them all to a better place. Addressing Beloved she tells her: 'My plan was to take us all to the other side where my own ma'am is' [203]. Where Baby Suggs felt the need to 'beg God's pardon' for Sethe's actions, Sethe herself feels justified in what she did: she stresses her connection to Beloved and all her children, seeing them as one and the same, 'when I tell you you mine,' she says, 'I also mean I'm yours' [203].

In the following chapter we see inside Denver's mind, and learn that she has always been afraid of Sethe, fearing that she might murder her too; she would try her best to please her in order to stay safe. We see her thoughts and opinions about her father Halle, who she has only heard of from others, and about her grandmother Baby Suggs. The latter once told her that what she feared most in the world was being beaten by whites in front of her children because she thought it might send them crazy. Grandma Suggs told her that her father never witnessed this, and so Denver assumes that he never went crazy. This is ironic because the reader knows from Paul D that Halle *did* eventually lose his mind after seeing Sethe abused. Denver dreams of her father returning home and looking after her and Beloved; she would be happy if it was just the three of them and if Sethe and Paul left 124. Like Sethe Denver is resentful of her mother, then, and the absence of a stable family has clearly had a profoundly negative effect on her. This chapter also underscores her connection to Beloved; when Beloved haunted the house Baby Suggs assured Denver that the ghost would never hurt her: they have a common bond because Denver she drank Beloved's blood at Sethe's breast; also the ghost has nothing to reproach Denver for; rather it is Sethe and Baby Suggs who are the focus of its resentment. Thus Denver feels that all Beloved needs from her is love, which she intends to give her, and she makes the same statement of ownership that Sethe made in the previous chapter: 'Beloved. She's mine' [209]. The idea of Denver drinking Beloved's blood suggests a possible link between her and the Christian tradition of the Eucharist, and Jesus's invitation for followers to partake of his body and blood. This in turn implies that we might think of Beloved as a saviour figure whose death is symbolic: she died so that the other children could remain alive, and free.

Chapter twenty two is told from Beloved's perspective and it is an extremely fragmented narrative, hinting at events without ever fully contextualizing them. It seems to relate the experiences of Beloved on a slave ship: the white slave traders are described as men without faces, and there are references to a life with her mother before the white men captured them. Life on the ship is horrific in the extreme, with bodies crammed together in the vessel and people dying and being shoved overboard. Her own mother—who she describes as a woman with her face—commits suicide because she cannot endure it. Slave ship crossings of this kind were truly horrific, and Morrison dedicates her novel to the 'Sixty Million and more' people who are thought to have perished during what is termed the Middle Passage from Africa to America. As suggested, it is difficult to know if we should see these slave ship memories as recording something that Beloved literally experienced, or whether it implies that she is tapping into the collective memory of those who suffered in this way. Or perhaps these memories relate to a timeless spirit world that Beloved knew prior to her reincarnation? It is not certain either if the person she refers to as her mother is actually Sethe, or whether Sethe comes to take the place of Beloved's lost mother. Certainly Beloved feels that Sethe is indeed her mother, and the chapter begins with another statement of possession: 'I AM BELOVED AND SHE IS MINE.' Her insistence that she is not separate from her mother brings to mind Sethe's feeling that her children are part of herself.

Beloved restates her connection to Sethe in chapter twenty three where she associates her with the woman who picked flowers before being taken to the slave ship. Here the voices of Beloved, Sethe and Denver are presented together: Sethe asks Beloved to forgive her but does not get a reply, and Denver seems to warn Beloved about Sethe, a warning that reflects her own suspicion of her mother. Later in the chapter the interacting voices are presented in the form of a poem, merging in the final stanzas until it becomes impossible to differentiate between them, and the chapter closes with the triple repetition of the line 'You are mine'. We cannot disentangle the voices and hence the characters' identities become indistinguishable; in a manner of speaking this merging of identity is also a loss of identity, and it is hard for the reader to feel positive about it. Indeed it seems clear that the relationship is unhealthy and unsustainable.

4.12 Chapters Twenty Four and Twenty Five

Having moved out of 124 Paul D took up residence in the church basement, and this chapter focuses on him. He reminisces about Sweet Home and the attempt to escape it. As suggested, life had been relatively good there before the arrival of schoolteacher: Mr Garner treated them with what seemed like respect, insisting that his slaves were men. When schoolteacher took over it seemed that he 'broke into children what Garner had raised into men' [220]. Now he is older Paul wonders whether he was ever a real man under slavery, even the benign variety practiced by Garner. Was he only a man because Garner granted him the privilege? And what was that privilege worth if it only applied on Sweet Home and could be taken away at any time? Paul's opinion of Sixo and Halle was that they were men regardless of Garner's say so, but he was unsure if he could say the same about himself.

When schoolteacher's cruelty becomes intolerable the slaves formulate a plan of escape. Sixo's Thirty Mile Woman tells him of party escaping North to the free states, and they all decide to accompany him: Pauls A and D, Halle, Sethe and her children. It is not completely clear why the plan fails, although Paul D speculates about the possibility of schoolteacher sensing anxiety in Halle's voice. Sixo and Paul D are captured, and when schoolteacher's men bind them

Sixo tries to escape, grabbing one of the men's rifles, singing as he does so. He hits one, but cannot position the rifle to defend himself: the whites watch him struggle until one of them knocks him out. Though initially schoolteacher wanted to take him alive this incident convinces him that Sixo is inherently rebellious and hence too much trouble. Paul D wonders if it was the singing that convinced him that Sixo was ungovernable, suggesting a link between music and freedom, and reinforcing our sense of the importance of music in the book. Either way schoolteacher decides to burn Sixo alive, but even as he's burning Sixo continues his rebellion: he begins laughing and shouting 'Seven–O! Seven–O!' which is a reference to the fact that his Thirty Mile Woman has escaped, pregnant with his child. While Sixo burns he celebrates the fact that part of him has escaped in the form of his unborn child, Seven–O. Thus Sixo remains rebellious to the last and his irrepressible spirit will live on in his offspring. In one sense at least it was impossible to make a slave out of Sixo, and perhaps it is this uncontrollable element in his character that lies behind Paul D's readiness to call him a man?

After Sixo is burned Paul D is returned to Sweet Home in a collar and shackles. When he tells Sethe about the failure of the plan she decides to make a run for it but is intercepted by schoolteacher's nephews. Amid all the horror, one of the things that strikes Paul most powerfully is his status as a commodity. At one point he overhears schoolteacher discussing the slaves as if they are livestock, referring to Sethe as 'the breeding one' and to her children as foal; he also learns the price of his own life: $900, which is the amount that schoolteacher thinks he can sell him for.

In the following chapter Stamp finds Paul D in the church and the two of them talk. He insists that Paul should be living with one of the black people in the community and names several who would take him in: the notion of mutual aid among blacks is extremely important to Stamp, as is the red ribbon he carries that belonged to the unknown black girl scalped by whites, and which he is seen handling in this chapter. The latter reminds him of the cruelty blacks have suffered at the hands of whites and it is interesting that he hides the ribbon when a white man arrives to ask him if he knows the whereabouts of a woman called Judy. The fact that Stamp pretends he doesn't know is indicative of the fear and suspicion white people arouse in him. In his conversation with Paul D we also learn more about why Stamp changed his name. His wife's abuse by the white man who slept with her lasted for many months and in all that time Stamp didn't make love her; when her ordeal with the white man was over Stamp wanted to break her neck, but he changed his name instead. As suggested the issue of name changing is important in *Beloved*: just like Baby Suggs, Stamp refuses to retain his given name, and the ability to change it suggests a degree of empowerment that is crucial for an ex-slave; it challenges schoolteacher's point that definitions belong to the definers. Stamp, like Baby Suggs, demonstrates the liberating potential of self-definition.

Stamp tells Paul D that he was present when Sethe killed Beloved, and he tries to defend her on the grounds that she loved her children and 'was trying to out-hurt the hurter.' Paul says that he is frightened of Sethe, but is even more frightened of Beloved. As they discuss her Stamp speculates about the possibility that she is a girl who escaped from a white man the previous summer, but Paul seems to feel there is something unnatural about her; she reminds him of something he 'is supposed to remember' [234], and he thinks she is a bitch. The chapter closes with a lament from Paul about the extent of his suffering over the years, and he asks Stamp how much he as a black man is supposed to endure. 'All he can,' says Stamp; this does not answer Paul's question, and the chapter closes with him reiterating the word 'Why?' five times.

Part Three

4.13 Chapters Twenty Six, Seven, and Eight

The relationship between Denver, Sethe and Beloved begins to deteriorate in their isolation at 124: Beloved becomes more demanding and Sethe, seemingly bewitched by her, is obsessed with trying to please her. For the most part Denver is ignored as Sethe and Beloved are fixated with one another in a relationship that excludes the outside world. Sethe loses her job and degrades herself in the way she panders to Beloved's demands. Eventually these are accompanied by accusations as Beloved tries to punish Sethe for abandoning her. Sethe pleads with her to understand that she planned for herself and her children to be together on the other side, but Beloved is deaf to this, reiterating the slave ship torments that were narrated in chapter twenty two: she is convinced that Sethe is the mother who left her, and she blames her for everything. Whenever Sethe tries to resist or confront Beloved she becomes violent, and as food grows scarce and Denver and Sethe starve, Beloved seems to get fatter. Denver hears her mother's attempts to justify herself to Beloved and begins to develop a broader perspective on the events. Where once she wanted to protect Beloved from Sethe, the opposite is now the case; she fears for her mother and decides that it is up to her to do something about the situation. This is hard because she has not really left 124 since she was seven years old, and the only two people she vaguely knows are Stamp Paid and Lady Jones. She decides to seek out Lady Jones, offering to work in exchange for food. Lady Jones cannot provide work, but offers Denver weekly reading lessons, and mentions Sethe's plight to the women at her church. Soon baskets of food begin appearing outside124 and Denver slowly gets to know the local community as she returns the baskets to their donors. The situation at home deteriorates further and Denver realises that she needs to get a job and so approaches the Bodwins for help. The Bodwins are ex-abolitionists and Mr Bodwin helped Sethe after she was charged with murder; however, at their house Denver sees a racist piggy bank cast in the shape of a stereotypical black slave, kneeling above the words 'At Yo' Service.' This reveals the latent racism existing even among liberal people like the Bodwins; their ignorance qualifies their progressive views and reveals the subtle, insidious forms that racism can take.

The Bodwin's servant Janey spreads the story of Beloved around the community, and when Stamp's fellow Underground Railroad agent, Ella, hears of Sethe's plight she decides to help. Ella, who was once held captive and repeatedly raped by a white father and son, understands the anger that made Sethe kill her daughter. While she cannot condone the act itself, she is infuriated at the idea of 'past errors taking possession of the present' [256], and so she rallies a group of black women in support of Sethe. A group of thirty descend on 124 and begin praying and singing. This becomes a kind of exorcism in which all of the black people present confront their past demons, particularly Ella with her history of extreme abuse. When Beloved appears on the porch she is naked and pregnant, and the women think she is the devil in the shape of a beautiful black woman. Sethe is stirred by the communal song because it has a spiritual dimension that reminds her of Baby Suggs at the Clearing. At this point Mr Bodwin arrives to pick up Denver to take her to work and when Sethe sees him she has a flashback to the day schoolteacher arrived. Mistaking Bodwin for schoolteacher, Sethe again feels the hummingbirds' 'needle beaks right through her headcloth into her hair,' and she flies at him with an ice pick [262].

The chapter closes from Beloved's perspective: she sees Sethe run, and Denver too; she sees all of the black people and Bodwin—a white man with a whip in his hand—elevated above them all. She refers to him as 'man without skin [who] is looking at her;' in other words the scene seems to conjure memories of her slave ship trauma, and the time when she was abandoned by her mother. Read in this way it might account for Beloved's flight at the end: she runs away from the scene at 124 because it seems that history is repeating itself.

In the next chapter Paul D and Stamp Paid discuss the events at 124: it appears that Sethe tried to murder Bodwin but Ella and the other women were able to subdue her. When Sethe mistook Bodwin for schoolteacher she attacked him rather than her children, which implies a change of mindset on her part: Sethe now feels the appropriate response is fight rather than flight, suggesting perhaps that conflicts need to be addressed in this world rather than the next.

Paul D feels certain that Beloved has now gone because the dog, Here Boy, has returned to 124. No one really knows what happened to her: she just seemed to disappear, although a boy claimed to have seen a naked woman running through the woods that day with 'fish for hair.' The exorcism has been successful, then, which suggests the positive potential of community: the ghost of the past is dismissed only when black people work together. To do this they have had to get over their past antagonism toward Sethe, and their actions to some extent atone for their failure to warn of schoolteacher's arrival eighteen years earlier.

Sethe is completely shattered by the events, and at the close of the novel has reached an emotional nadir. Paul D goes to see her and gives her assurance that he will help her recover, praising her in a way that shows his respect for her despite his former misgivings. It hints that the two of them might have a future together and their story ends on a positive note in this respect. The fact that Paul is there to help means he remembers his promise to assist Sethe's terrifying journey inside herself.

While Sethe regressed to the status of a child under the spell of Beloved, Denver has matured. When Paul D met her on his way to 124 there was none of her former hostility. The final weeks in 124 have been a salutary experience for her, forcing her to take responsibility for herself and her mother. She is now working for Miss Bodwin, and there is a possibility that she might be able to go to college. Denver has a future, then, and this is significant not just for her but for African Americans generally: the fact that someone from Denver's background can look forward with any degree of optimism implies that the things might be improving after all. In some respects Denver represents the promise and potential of African American people: she has the intelligence and strength of character required to overcome the obstacles that stopped her engaging with the world. Where her mother was inhibited by the past and could only look backwards, Denver is able to think of the future. The fact that Beloved's dress still hangs on a peg in 124, however, implies that Beloved and all that she represents cannot easily be forgotten.

The final chapter hints at how Beloved might be remembered. The refrain throughout the piece is that 'It was not a story to pass on', which implies that it might be best to forget Beloved. Some of the townsfolk traded stories about what happened at 124 and then 'quickly and deliberately forgot her,' because 'Remembering seemed unwise' [274]. It is difficult to see how it is possible to deliberately forget something, however, and statements like this have to be read in relation to the role that Beloved has played as a catalyst for remembering. Her appearance has forced Sethe and Paul D—indeed the whole community—to remember and engage with the past. The line, 'What made her think her fingernails could open locks the rain rained on?' is undermined by the fact that this is exactly what she *has* done: she has unlocked the past for those characters who knew her, even though this past was painful to recall. This contradiction suggests that while there are things that black people may want to forget, it might be in their interest to remember; however, perhaps it suggests also that what Beloved represents should be remembered, but not dwelt on. Remembering and acknowledging the significance of the past is positive and essential, but obsessing about it is generally a mistake. Likewise the idea that this is 'not a story to pass on' is undermined by the book itself: the story *has* been passed on because we are holding it in our hands. The words seem to imply that it is hard to pass it on, *not* that it shouldn't be passed on. Beloved all but disappears from the memory—just like the anonymous 'sixty million and more' who died during the Middle Passage—but in a sense she demands to be remembered. She *should be* remembered, and the novel insists on doing so, underscoring this fact by closing the novel with her name positioned as the final paragraph: Beloved.

5. Interpreting Beloved

Beloved has attracted a vast amount of scholarship since its publication and it has been read in a variety of ways. This section considers some of the most illuminating approaches to the text and the important contexts within which it has been read. Morrison has stressed that there is no one way to read the novel, and when it comes to the status of Beloved herself, readers must ask the questions that the book's characters are forced to ask: such questions may have multiple or even contradictory answers, and readers should approach this fascinating novel, and those critics who strive to make sense of it, with this in mind.

5.1 Beloved and Modernism

Modernism is a cultural phenomenon linked to the early part of the twentieth century, and though it was largely over before Toni Morrison was even born, her work is sometimes associated with a modernist aesthetic. The term is most often used to refer to the ways artists responded to the social and intellectual changes of the period. By the early twentieth century many of the assumptions people had had about who they were, where they came from, and how they relate to one another had been challenged; for instance, people like Charles Darwin (1809–1882), Friedrich Nietzsche (1844–1900), Sigmund Freud (1856–1939), Karl Marx (1818–1883), among others challenged long held beliefs about human origin, character, morality, autonomy, and perception, effectively making the world seem a much more complicated place than it had previously appeared. Also new technologies changed how people related to the world: modes of mass communication like radio and cinema played an increasing part in life, offering new insights and perspectives. The Western world— American and Europe—was becoming increasingly urbanised too, and many found city life disorientating and disaffecting. Also WWI had a huge impact on people: this was the first war in which human-kind's destructive potential really became evident on a huge scale, again facilitated by new technologies. The horror of WWI is often felt to underpin the psychic trauma seen in modernist art, which is often about angst and alienation. In the light of these changes to people's understanding of the world, traditional realism no longer seemed ade-quate for conveying it: the new world demanded new ways of seeing and communicating. Some of the techniques associated with mod-ernist aesthetics, for instance, include stream of consciousness nar-rative offering subjective points-of-view that reflect how the world is unknowable beyond limited perspectives. Also fragmented and disjointed narratives register the uncertainty people felt about real-ity, and the feeling that coherent identity—people's sense of them-selves as integrated individuals—was under threat. Modernism is often informed by a craving for unity in the face of this perceived disintegration.

However, some argue that this view of modernism betrays a lim-ited reading of history which privileges Western perspectives over African culture. Cynthia Dobbs, for instance, argues that for Africans and African Americans 'this moment of cultural and personal disso-lution occurs' much earlier than the twentieth century.[1] She argues that slavery caused psychological and social disruption in the lives of African Americans that precipitated a suspicion of realism akin to that associated with modernism; she claims that African art actually constitutes a form of modernism that predates the Western variety by decades. For Dobbs, Morrison 'revisits' these modernist themes and aesthetics in *Beloved*.

Dobbs argues that, as with modernist authors, Morrison often acknowledges the limits of language. For African Americans who have suffered slavery there are things that conventional language simply cannot communicate. For example in Baby Suggs's sermon there comes a point where she stops talking and continues to convey her message through dance: we are told that she dances 'with her twisted hip the rest of what her heart had to say' [Dobbs, 566]. Baby

---

1   Cynthia Dobbs. '*Beloved*: Bodies Returned, Modernism Revisited.' *African American Review*, 32, 4, 1998: 563–578. 563.

Suggs begins to dance to music provided by her audience and the speech becomes less like a conventional oration and more like an interactive event. The orator and the crowd are drawn together in what Dobbs refers to as a 'state of grace' and 'a shared sense of 'personal imagination and responsibility.' This has redemptive and unifying possibilities for the community, potentially combating the feelings of disintegration occasioned by slavery. The desire for unity is a key characteristic of modernism, and it can be seen again at the end of the novel where the community of women help Sethe deal with Beloved. At first the women are described as praying in a conventional way, but then we are told that they 'stopped praying and took a step back to the beginning. In the beginning there were no words. In the beginning there was sound, and they all knew what that sound sounded like' [Dobbs, 566]. Here Morrison presents sound as superior to words, and according to Dobbs this implies

> a sort of pre-linguistic unity, evincing what we recognise as modernist longing for a lost moment of wholeness, while also placing this moment within the context of African American spirituality and music [Dobbs, 567].

So the craving for unity has modernist associations, as does the non-conventional, non-linguistic means of achieving it.

Conventional modes of communication are also inadequate for Paul D's chain gang in Alfred, Georgia. The prisoners are not allowed to speak on pain of death so they turn to the 'rhythms of music and movement in order to express their rage and sorrow.' Again they create their own way of communicating in a context where words are inadequate, and this proves effective: in this way they achieve freedom during the flood when 'they "talk through that chain" that binds all forty-six together, wordlessly coordinating a group escape' [Dobbs, 567]. This kind of communication is difficult to reconcile with traditional realism: it embodies the spirit of modernism, but it has its origins in *African* culture rather than Western culture; as Dobbs points out:

> Morrison's achievement is both to reveal the limitations and assumptions of the "American vocabulary" and [...] do a neces-

sary "great violence" to conventional language, opening it up to the syntax and stories of African American culture and history— a mode of emphatically modernist narrative' [Dobbs, 568].

In other words she exposes the limits of realism and creates a space for less conventional modes of narration. More importantly, the modernist aspects of *Beloved* have an African origin, and in demonstrating this the novel makes an important cultural point.

Further disruption to convention can be seen in the novel's attitude to memory and how the past relates to the present. Sethe's notion of rememory suggests that the past is always present and, according to Dobbs, this implies a 'modernist foregrounding of memory as [...] subjective and unstable.' The memory that haunts the ex-slaves principally, of course, is their history of slavery, and this creates trauma akin to that which underpinned modernism in the West. For African Americans slavery is linked to feelings of psychological and literal disintegration: psychic trauma precludes Sethe and Paul D becoming fully integrated characters, of course, and during their time as slaves literal disintegration was a very real prospect given that they lived under constant threat to their lives. A terror of disintegration and dissolution is central to modernism, as is the yearning for wholeness mentioned above, and it registers clearly in the two stream of consciousness chapters where Beloved expresses her memory of the Middle Passage. Dobbs shows how in chapter twenty two Beloved and Sethe seem to merge: there is very little difference between their identities, a fact underscored by the absence of punctuation and lack of syntactic distinction between the two women. Consider this quote:

> I am Beloved and she is mine. I see her take flowers away from leaves she puts them in a round basket the leaves are not for her she fills the basket she opens the grass I would help but the clouds are in the way how can I see things that are pictures I am not separate from her there is no place where I stop her face is my own and I want to be there in the face where her face is and to be looking at it too [quoted in Dobbs, 570].

The notion that Sethe and Beloved's identities are blurred here is conveyed explicitly ('I am not separate from her'), but it is further reinforced by the fact that the sentences, like the characters, have no boundaries. References to the collapsing of identity are set against images of slave ship horror: the bodies piled high on the ship, the suicides, the suffocating atmosphere, and so on. These images are conveyed in a similar fragmented, stream of consciousness way which for Dobbs implies a breakdown of language: again conventional modes of communication are rendered inadequate by the subject. Beloved's longing for unity with the mother is inexpressible in language since language depends on difference for meaning (words only have meaning because they are different from other words), and so language cannot convey the kind of unity Beloved desires and seeks to express; likewise the nightmare of the slave ship is also inexpressible in language because 'the horrors to the body seem beyond the powers of the imagination and language to contain' [Dobbs, 572]. The experience of the Middle Passage—an experience central to African American history—can only be addressed via modernist aesthetics, not via traditional realism. Dobbs goes on to observe that the following chapter is more conventional in the way it is presented, at least in the first paragraph: here there are more fully formed coherent sentences, and where the first chapter blurred the identities of Beloved and Sethe, these two characters are now seen as separate entities: Beloved uses Sethe's name to describe her rather than a pronoun, and there are much clearer distinctions between the two woman. Here Morrison seems to remake the world in a way that allows for distinct identities; according to Dobbs this suggests progression and the redemptive potential of remembering or reconstructing the past. However, the fact that the identities merge again at the close of the chapter when the narrative takes the form of poetry seems to qualify Dobbs' argument to some degree.

The idea that some things are unsayable in language brings us back to music, particularly the jazz aesthetic discussed earlier in this book. Jazz has affinities with modernism and Morrison herself alludes to these in interview: 'Music makes you hungry for more of it. It never really gives you the whole number. It slaps and it embraces, it slaps and it embraces' [Quoted in Dobbs, 574]. Like modernism, jazz avoids closure; it is evasive and contradictory, and *Beloved* shares these characteristics. For instance, Dobbs argues that the 'slap and embrace' spirit of jazz can be seen in the way *Beloved* juxtaposes horror and beauty. The language of the prose is very often lyrical but this lyricism is at odds with the horror of its subject. One example might be the beauty of the scars that Sethe has on her back: they take the form of a chokecherry tree, and are described in prose that is rich and poetic: the 'slap' of the horrific incident is redressed by the 'embrace' of the lyricism used to describe it. Moreover there is a slap and an embrace at the heart of the book's depiction of disintegration and dissolution on the one hand, and the possibility of unity on the other: the 'slap' of the breakdown of identity and community under slavery, and the 'embrace' of the integration and unity that is suggested at the end of the book. Given that jazz is underpinned principally by black musical rhythms, this again links *Beloved* to a modernism which is African rather than Western in origin.

5.2 Beloved and Postmodernism

Though it has affinities with modernism, *Beloved* is most often discussed in relation to postmodernism, a cultural phenomenon associated with the latter part of the twentieth century. In the early days of Morrison's writing career, some postmodern theorists—most notably Fredric Jameson and Jean Baudrillard—were pointing out the inaccessibility of history. The only history we have comes in the form of narratives that distort it: at best we have an approximation of history, at worst a deceptive notion of the past built around reductive stereotypes. Increasingly our experience seems confined to the present, cut-off from an unknowable past. One reading of the postmodern attitude is that the past is being forgotten or ignored as a result of this perceived inaccessibility. However, other theorists have noticed that, conversely, postmodern art engages with history. Linda Hutcheon, for instance, identified what she calls historiographic metafiction as a type of postmodern narrative that exposes the shortcomings of traditional history and re-engages us with the past in a more critical and informed way. Kimberly Chabot Davis is one of the first critics to discuss *Beloved* in relation to these issues, and her account will be discussed here.

In one sense Toni Morrison seems to embrace postmodernism's scepticism of history: for instance she feels that 'history is always fictional;'[1] however, at the same time she considers herself to be an author of social protest, and hence the idea of reliable history is important to her: if she is to affect change in the lives of African Americans then their history of discrimination must be recalled and interrogated. Davis suggests that *Beloved* is a 'hybrid' novel that, in the spirit of postmodernism, acknowledges that history is impossible to know in an absolute way, but which nevertheless reclaims alternative histories on behalf of African American people. Thus, 'although Morrison demystifies master historical narratives, she also wants to raise 'real' or authentic African American history in its place. She deconstructs while she reconstructs'[Chabot Davies 245]. So Morrison challenges traditional representations of history, wishing to explore previously marginalised black perspectives on the past. Her approach to history is linked to her attitude to art. She does not see a difference between fiction and history, and she feels that artists are the best placed among us to reconstruct history in a meaningful way: for Morrison artists are the 'truest historians,' despite dealing in fiction not facts. Her purpose in *Beloved* was to convey Margaret Garner's story in a way that gave it meaning and power in relation to a lived experience, rather than just as a documented event: she was '"giving blood to the scraps [...] and a heartbeat" to what had been merely a historical curio' [Chabot Davis, 245].

Part of Morrison's method has to do with showing how perspective differs for black people: for instance, from a twentieth century white perspective the key event of early 1860s America would have been the Civil War, but notice how little this features in the lives of the characters in *Beloved*. When Denver mentions 'the war years' it is in relation to the cologne she received as a gift at that time; the details of the war itself don't register. Similarly, while Paul D participated in the war, the reader hardly hears anything about it: his war memories seem to have been eclipsed by his experiences on the chain

---

1   Kimberly Chabot Davis, 'Postmodern Blackness: Toni Morrison's *Beloved* and the End of History.' *Twentieth Century Literature*, 44, 2, 1998: 242–260. 243

gang in Alfred. In other words *his* history, his own personal experiences mean more to him than the grand event. In this sense 'Morrison attempts to redefine history as an amalgamation of local narratives' [Chabot Davis 246], demonstrating that history isn't a single narrative, more a collage of perspectives.

At the same time Morrison acknowledges that all history distorts the past. When Paul D comes across the newspaper accounts of Sethe's trial after killing Beloved, he feels that there is a mismatch between what he sees in the paper and what he knows from experience: 'that ain't her mouth,' he says. Here Morrison makes the point that documents don't make history: history can never be adequately conveyed in a text or a photograph. However, at the same time she concedes that history is only available via the texts that distort it, making reference to the newspapers being stored in the woodshed, the very place where Sethe killed Beloved; for Davis these papers become 'the metaphoric spectres to the 'real' action of this fictional story' [Chabot Davis, 248]. So while Morrison deems it important to explore the past she also acknowledges that it cannot be fully known, and indeed sometimes there are aspects of the past that must be jettisoned in order for people to be happy and move forward. Hence while the novel is partly about exploring and confronting the past, we are also told that 'it was not a story to pass on.' As Davis says:

> although Morrison promotes delving into the historical past, she realizes that the past must be processed and sometimes forgotten in order for one to function in the present and 'pass on' to the future [Chabot Davis, 250]

Davis sees this as indication that *Beloved* is mid-way between 'traditional historical remembering and postmodernist forgetting of the past,' and thus an example of a 'hybrid' novel incorporating aspects of both realism and postmodernism [Chabot Davis, 250].

Beloved also demonstrates how individuals are complicit in making history. Sethe, for instance, is troubled by the fact that she made the ink that allowed schoolteacher to record what he sees as her 'animal characteristics.' She can never alter the fact that she did this and as such is part of the making of history herself. Thus while we might explore the past and seek a better understanding of it, there is always a sense in which we produce it—even those aspects we may wish to erase or remake—and are invariably implicated in it.

While modernism craves unity, postmodernism acknowledges its impossibility and *Beloved* might be seen as postmodern in this sense: it suggests that history is never complete, that it is impossible to offer a comprehensive history in narrative form. There will always be untold stories, marginalised and omitted perspectives. The gaps that Morrison leaves in the story make this point of course. Thus while Sethe's sons, Howard and Buglar, feature at the beginning of the novel, their story is not told, and neither is Halle's. These deliberate loose ends are suggestive of the countless unrecorded histories we cannot know. Also some sections of the book are deliberately oblique: for example the Middle Passage section is presented in an elliptical, fragmented way which stresses the inaccessibility of that experience for anyone other than those who suffered it first-hand. Indeed *Beloved* as a whole resists narrative closure: the figure of Beloved is deliberately ambiguous, and her status is unresolved at the close of the novel. All of these things suggest a postmodern conception of history, but, as Davis insists, the book is intent on rethinking rather than ignoring history, so while it wants to question and problematize history, it does not want to us lose sight of its importance. In other words if we are to call *Beloved* postmodern then it is in the sense that Linda Hutcheon uses the term: in keeping with her concept of historiographical metafiction, it is a *revision* of history rather than a dismissal of history.

The conception of time is also non-conventional in *Beloved* of course. Time is presented as non-linear, with the past perpetually intruding on the present: Sethe maintains that the past never goes away; her notion of rememory implying that things have a potential permanence in the world. This non-linear view of time is in the tradition of postmodernism too in that it denies the possibility of closure, and refuses to be reduced to a predictable narrative trajectory. Arguably this notion of time as has its origins in African culture which is less bound by Western ideas of chronology and structure. Thus, as with the discussion of modernism, there is a sense in which the book could be seen as simply *African* American rather than postmodern, drawing influences from the heritage of the people at the heart of the story. While the term postmodern is applicable, then, the characteristics that allow critics to use it are apposite to its African American origins.

5.3 Beloved and Realism

The question of whether Beloved is a ghost or not has often been debated, with most critics viewing her as a magical reincarnation of Sethe's murdered daughter, the return of her repressed past. In turn this reincarnation becomes symbolic of African American repression of the psychic pain of former enslavement. Some argue that it is not necessary to see a supernatural element in *Beloved*, however, and that the character's appearance at 124 can be explained without reference to the paranormal. One of the most notable critics to make this point is Elizabeth E. House in her article, 'Toni Morrison's Ghost: The Beloved Who Is Not Beloved.' House sees significance in the preface to the novel which is a quotation from the Bible, Romans 9:25: 'I will call them my people, who are not my people; and her beloved, which was not beloved.' She argues that this hints that Sethe and Denver are wrong to see Beloved as Sethe's murdered daughter. The name of this woman is Beloved, but she is a different Beloved; as in the quotation she calls them—and they call her—'my people,' but they are not. House supports her argument mainly with reference to chapters twenty two and three where Beloved describes the Middle Passage experience. She interprets these stream of consciousness sections rather like a poem in which Beloved weaves together images and references that hint at her origins, albeit it in a puzzling way. It tells the story of a girl who is taken with her mother by white slave traders—'men without skin'—from her home in Africa. The mother is picking flowers when they come; the daughter wanted to help her but she was blinded by gunsmoke and lost sight of her. Beloved says that she loses her mother three times:

> 'Three times I lost her: once with the flowers because of the noisy clouds of smoke; once when she went into the sea instead of smiling at me; once under the bridge when I went to join her

and she came towards me but did not smile.'[1]

House argues that these three occasions on which Beloved loses her mother structure her experiences throughout these chapters. The first occasion is when the slave traders take her away on capturing them in Africa, after which Beloved finds herself on a slave ship. The conditions are horrific and death so common that the slave traders push corpses through portholes with poles. She identifies a man who may be her father but he soon dies. She knows her mother—'the woman with my face'—is very distressed: she has lost the diamond earrings she used to wear and these have been replaced by an iron collar around her neck. Beloved tells us that her mother 'does not like it', and so she wants to 'bite it away' in order to set her free. She senses that her mother 'wants her earrings' back together with the 'round basket' in which she collected her flowers at home in Africa. At one point on the ship Beloved thinks her mother is about to smile at her but instead she throws herself overboard because she cannot bear the horror of the ship any longer. This is the second traumatic separation for Beloved: just as she thought she was going to be shown some affection her mother leaves her; Beloved tries to follow her but is trapped in the crush of bodies on the ship: 'I wanted to join her in the sea but I could not move.' She has been abandoned again. Later, some of the other slaves are taken from the ship but Beloved herself remains, and comes under the control of an officers who sexually abuses her; she tells us that 'he hurts where I sleep,' and 'puts his finger there.' The man calls her Beloved when he is abusing her and this is how she gets her name. She makes references to waiting on a bridge because she thinks her mother is under it, and House speculates whether this may be the bridge of the ship on which she is captive: her mother is below the ship in the sea, the place where she last saw her, and in this sense she is beneath the ship's bridge. Then there is a shift forward in time and Beloved is relocated from the ship to the creek at the rear of 124. There is no indication of how she arrived there but House sees enough evidence to suggest that she

1   Elizabeth E. House 'Toni Morrison's Ghost: The Beloved Who Is Not Beloved.' In Solomon, Barbara H. Critical Essays on Toni Morrison's Beloved. (New York: G.K. Hall & Co, 1998) 117–126. 119

could have escaped from the man who had been holding her captive as a sex slave. She tells Denver that she had been in a house with a white man who had hurt her, of course, and at one point Stamp Paid makes reference to a man who has been found dead nearby: he had been keeping a girl captive, but there was no sign of her. It is difficult to know why Morrison would include these details if not to point the reader in this direction. Of course if Beloved had been kept captive in this way then that would account for her strange behaviour: she would have had little opportunity to learn how to use language properly, or to develop social skills. Also the fact that Beloved's skin is so smooth might indicate that she has been indoors for a very long period. Thus the escaped Beloved arrives at the creek behind 124, profoundly traumatised, and still fixated on the mother that she has lost. In the creek Beloved thinks she sees diamonds, and this could be sun sparkling in the water; Beloved associates this with her lost mother's diamond earrings. Looking into the creek she sees her own reflection and immediately identifies this as her mother too (she has been described as having her face of course). Beloved last saw her mother in water, and House suggests that 'to the untutored girl, all bodies of water are connected as one' [House 121]. She dives into the water but obviously cannot make a connection with her imaginary mother, and this constitutes the third loss of her mother. Following these losses she immediately makes the connection with her vanished birth mother when she sees Sethe: 'Sethe is the one that picked flowers [...] in the place before the crouching [...] Sethe went into the sea' [House 121]. So this suggests that Beloved can be seen as a 'real' person and there is no supernatural connection to Sethe; her obsession is born of the loss of her actual birth mother.

This reading of Beloved as real person fits well with other episodes in the book. When Sethe, Denver and Beloved are in the Clearing and Sethe begins to choke, Denver accuses Beloved of being the cause. However, Beloved replies: 'I didn't choke it. The circle of iron choked it,' which alludes to the slave collar that her dead mother was forced to wear. Beloved's apparent knowledge of Sethe's earrings makes Sethe suspect that she is her daughter, but again her questioning can be explained by her memory of her real mother's stolen diamonds. Similarly Beloved's responses to Denver's questions about what life was like in the 'other world' suggest a slave ship experience rather than a reference to the afterlife: 'Hot. Nothing to breathe down there and no room to move in' [House 123]. Later when Sethe asks her if she comes from 'from the other side,' and Beloved answers yes, she could obviously mean Africa rather than the spirit world. At the end of the novel when the community drive Beloved out, she witnesses a series of events which recall the loss of her real mother. She sees Sethe running away from her just as her own mother had done, 'joining them' as her own mother had joined those who had gone overboard on the slave ship. Beloved is once more 'Alone,' and so runs away herself, fearful again of what a future without her mother might have in store.

House points out that it is historically possible for a girl of Beloved's age to have made a slave ship crossing. Despite a slave trade blockade, ships were still making the crossing illegally during the 1850s; alternatively, she could have found her way to North America via South America, which was still receiving slave traffic at this time. This would explain her line 'the others who are taken I am not taken': it could imply that while the majority of slaves were unloaded in South America, the pretty Beloved was kept on by an officer and brought to America by him for his own pleasure.

It is worth noting too that before Beloved arrives there has been a carnival in town exhibiting the usual array of fairground absurdities and freaks such as two headed people and giants. The narrator tells us that, 'the fact that none of it was true did not extinguish their appetite for it one bit '[House 126]. This makes an obvious point about people's willingness to believe in things that aren't true, perhaps suggesting that Sethe, Denver, and Beloved are, like everyone, prone to give credence to things that should be treated with scepticism. In this case, of course, the false identifications they make fulfil a need born of loss and trauma.

So how might this view of Beloved as a 'real person' influence our reading of the novel? How would it change what this character represents in relation to the primary themes of the book? If we allow this alternative version of Beloved's history then there is a sense in which she would have been the last remaining slave in America, kept until 1873, eight years after slavery was formally abolished. Thus she arrives in the town as a recent slave among a community of ex-slaves, and can still be seen to represent the traumatic past coming to haunt the present: into this community of ex-slaves struggling to repress the past comes a recent slave; she returns, not from death as Sethe's daughter, but from slavery itself. In other words even if we think of Beloved as real she still signifies in the same way: she can still be seen to represent the return of the repressed, the phenomenon identified by Sigmund Freud whereby elements repressed in the unconscious refuse to go away and re-emerge in the conscious mind in occasionally oblique and destructive ways.

The novel refuses to confirm or deny Beloved's status, and the skilful way in which Morrison presents the character allows readers to interpret her in their own way. Indeed Morrison herself stresses the importance of seeing Beloved as both things at once. In interview with Marsha Darling she says:

> She is spirit on one hand, literally she is what Sethe thinks she is, her child returned to her from the dead. And she must function like that in the text. She is also another kind of dead which is not spiritual but flesh, which is, a survivor from the true, factual slave ship […] both things are possible, and there's evidence in the text that both things could be approached, because the language of both experiences—death and the Middle Passage—is the same.[1]

This invites a non-hierarchical response to *Beloved* that refuses to privilege reality over the supernatural. Rather it insists that the two possibilities, like two ways of seeing the world, can exist simultaneously, each one enhancing rather than undermining the other.

5.4 Language and Motherhood in Beloved

Some of the most interesting critiques of *Beloved* focus Sethe's role as a mother and how her relationships with her children shape her

---

1   Darling, Marsha. 'In the Realm of Responsibility: A Conversation with Toni Morrison'. *Women's Review of Books* 5 (1988): 5–6.

thinking. One of the best known and most thought-provoking is Jean Wyatt's 'Giving Body to the Word', published in 1993. Wyatt takes a psychoanalytical approach which draws on Jacques Lacan's theory of language and identity. Lacan describes 'a child's entry into language as a move from maternal bodily connection to a register of abstract signifiers;'[1] in other words, initially a child sees no distinction between itself and its mother, but maturation requires entry into society and the world of language, which demands a recognition of the self as a separate entity. Once socialisation occurs the ability to think in terms of differences is essential: it is only the ability to perceive symbolic differences that makes meaning possible (words only have meaning because they are different from other words). Wyatt argues that Sethe's ability to perceive difference is unnaturally inhibited: she 'defines herself as a maternal body' who is unable to see a distinction between herself and her offspring; in this sense Sethe behaves like a pre-socialised infant, and her inability to perceive differences extends to her use of language: 'her insistence on her own physical presence and connection to her children precludes an easy acceptance of the separations and substitutions that govern language' [Wyatt 474]. Throughout the text Sethe struggles to describe her relationship with her children in ways that acknowledge their difference from her, and according to Wyatt this makes it impossible for her to engage with them or the world properly, and precludes the possibility of moving forward in her life.

Morrison presents Sethe in the tradition of the 'heroic slave mother' common to slave narratives such as Harriet Jacobs's *Incidents in the Life of a Slave Girl* (1861): in stories of this kind the female slave's principal motivation for escaping is to ensure her children's freedom, and Wyatt argues that this is the case with Sethe. She shows how Morrison's narrative does not really celebrate Sethe's freedom as such; rather it stresses the sense of connection between her and her children, and sees this alone as the benefit of freedom, and her prime achievement in escaping. Thus when discussing it with Paul D she says: 'I was big, Paul D, and deep and wide and when I stretched out

---

1   Jean Wyat, 'Giving Body to the Word: The Maternal Symbolic in Toni Morrison's *Beloved*.' *PMLA*, Vol. 108, No. 3 (May, 1993) 474–488. 475

my arms all my children could get in between. I was that wide,' and she tells him of how proud she was that 'she had milk enough for all' [Wyatt, 467]. Wyatt makes the point that 'even after the children are weaned, her bond with them remains so strong that she continues to think of it as a nursing connection' [Wyatt, 476]; Sethe's thinking is dominated by her perceived link to her children, and she exists only for their benefit. Moreover, Sethe's reluctance or inability to see a distinction between herself and her offspring underpins her decision to murder them when schoolteacher threatens to return them to slavery. It also makes it impossible for Sethe to put the act of murdering Beloved into words. When it comes to her children Sethe will not allow the separation—the acknowledgement of difference—that is a prerequisite of language and so she cannot find the words to articulate the act of murdering her child; Beloved *is* her, and so it is impossible for her conceptualise let alone express the notion of murder. When she tries to describe the incident she cannot engage with it: 'Sethe knew that the circle she was making around […] the subject would remain one. That she could never close in, pin it down for anybody who had to ask' [Wyatt, 476]. Sethe's overweening sense of connection to her children makes it difficult for her to 'accept the principle of substitution' necessary 'to invest in words,' and so she can only circle around the issue unable to speak it. Invoking Lacan, Wyatt writes:

> To move into a position in language and the social order, according to Lacan, an infant must sacrifice its imaginary sense of wholeness and continuity with the mother's body. (Sethe is of course in the mother's position rather than the child's, but her physical connection with her nursing baby resembles the infant's initial radical dependency on the mother's body.) [Wyatt 477]

This concept of language implies that something must be lost before it can be named: the signifier takes the place of the actual thing; as Lacan says, a signifier 'manifests itself first of all in the murder of the thing;' Sethe cannot commit such a murder because of the sense of oneness she feels: she cannot let go. Wyatt also quotes John Muller's contention that, 'the word destroys the immediacy of objects and gives us distance from them,' [Wyatt, 477] and argues that Sethe cannot tolerate such a distance and so cannot express Beloved's death in words. She cannot allow one thing to stand for another (which is how words work) and Wyatt shows how Sethe does not think in terms of metaphor where her children are concerned: as a result everything that would/should be dealt with figuratively and hence distanced from the self remains unmediated and perpetually present in Sethe's life. This presence takes its most obvious form in the physical manifestation of Beloved. Sethe cannot narrativise her murdered daughter because she cannot separate herself from her, so Beloved remains literally present, and of course gradually forces everything else from her life. Indeed, Wyatt observes a general reluctance for Sethe to substitute words for things, which makes it hard for her to detach herself, not just from her children, but from the past too. Her notion of rememory demonstrates how the past is always present for Sethe; her sense of connection to her absent child extends to the past, and she is reluctant to jettison that past just as she refuses to break the connection with Beloved. Sethe's world is clogged with baggage from which she cannot detach herself; in Wyatt's words: 'everything is there [in Sethe's life] in oppressive plenitude' [Wyatt 477]. This plenitude occupies everything in Sethe's world, thus when Paul D arrives at 124 there is *literally* no place for him: he has to create one with violence, driving the spirit of her dead child from the house. But when Beloved comes back she closes that space again and Paul D is side-lined.

Words cannot stand for things in Sethe's life and so her language and her thinking are often literal. This can be seen when Paul D cups her breasts when they are first reunited. Sethe feels as if she has been 'relieved of the weight of her breasts,' [Wyatt 478] and at first it looks as if this should be interpreted metaphorically, that it refers to Paul D assuming responsibility for Sethe's burden; the opposite is the case however, as Wyatt explains:

> When the maternal body becomes the locus of discourse, the metaphorical becomes the actual, a move that reinforces Sethe's definition of motherhood as an embodied responsibility: there are no substitutes, metaphorical or otherwise, for her breasts [Wyatt, 478].

Wyatt claims that the modifying words 'of her breasts' imply that we are meant to interpret the words literally rather than metaphorically: in other words she is relieved of her breasts rather than of her burden. Sethe's separation anxiety is reflected in the fact that she cannot engage in discourse normally; she cannot think normally, or relate to the world in a healthy way. Her concept of motherhood is such that it constitutes a burden that cannot be alleviated because nothing can substitute for it.

Sethe's inability to engage in metaphor and substitution means that she becomes defined by language, rather than able to use language to understand and perhaps come to terms with her own experience. This affects all aspects of her life and thought. Thus, for instance, she can only discuss her whipping scars in terms of Amy's description of them as a chokecherry tree. This is how she describes it when she talks about it with Paul D. She must use someone else's metaphor because she cannot address her own experience and suffering in her own way: she is incapable of detached reflection, evaluation and definition, and hence she remains defined by the slave master's inscription on her body.

In part two of the novel the unity between mother and daughter becomes more evident, and the lack of differentiation is manifest in language. The notion of possession suggested by the reiteration of the word 'mine' throughout chapters twenty to twenty three underscores this, for instance, as does the literal breakdown of coherence in some sections. Eventually it seems as if mother and daughter literally merge and it is no longer possible to know who is saying what. The words 'I have your milk/I brought your milk' are difficult to attach to a specific speaker: they could come from Sethe or Beloved; in Wyatt's words: 'the nursing connection erodes the distinctions of the symbolic by making the boundary between "you" and "me" soluble' [Wyatt, 481]. There is no differentiation between mother and daughter here, then, and the lack of distinction renders those words that usually confer distinction and individuality ('you' and 'me') redundant.

It is Denver who finally manages to break the destructive unity between Sethe and her children. She leaves 124 and seeks out Lady

Jones, significantly the woman who taught her to read. Lady Jones has access to a different kind of language—one associated with education and community, rather than the insular discourse that has characterised her relationship with Sethe and Beloved. At one point Lady Jones calls her 'baby' and this show of affection helps convey to Denver that she is 'a child of the community, not just her mother' [Wyatt, 483]. The social world is potentially nurturing but in order to enter it she must separate from the mother. As Wyatt explains:

> Denver moves into the symbolic by leaving one nurturing maternal circle for another, but there is a difference. The community, which operates as a network of mutual aid [...] demands instead a reciprocal nurturing. "To belong to a community of other free Negroes [is] to love and be loved by them [to] feed and be fed." Denver enters into this nurturing reciprocity, "pay[ing] a thank you for half a pie," "paying" for help by telling her story' [Wyatt, 483]

Social nurturing must replace maternal nurturing, and while the latter is inward-looking the former insists on engagement and reciprocity. Through this act of separation from Sethe Denver is able to move outward and forward in a way that has been denied so far.

The community intervenes on behalf of Sethe eventually: they exorcise Beloved and this creates the separation necessary for her also to recognise herself as an individual, and to potentially progress. When Beloved is finally expelled this recreates a space for Paul D both in 124 and Sethe's life. At the close of the book he tells her that she is her own 'best thing' and she answers, significantly, 'Me? Me?' The use of the first person pronoun is crucial because it demonstrates that Sethe does indeed have a sense of herself as separate. Wyatt sees significance too in Paul D's use of the words, 'You are' when addressing Sethe: it replaces the phrase 'You are mine' seen in the earlier chapter. While the former acknowledges the self the latter denies identity and separation; 'You are mine' is the phrase associated with ownership and slavery and is not the basis of a healthy relationship between mother and daughter, or indeed between any human beings.

> The hope at the end of the novel is that Sethe, having recognized herself as subject, will narrate the mother–daughter story and invent a language that can encompass the desperation of the slave mother who killed her daughter [Wyatt, 484]

This reading of *Beloved* suggests that Sethe is psychologically separate from her daughter at the end, and beginning to acknowledge herself as an entity apart from her children. Having finally achieved this she might now be in a position to make sense of her past and her actions, and find a way of expressing it.

5.5 Dissenting Voices

Almost all of the reviews to appear at the time of *Beloved*'s publication were positive, and subsequent evaluations mostly agree that it is a brilliant and important novel. However, as with all novels, there are those who feel differently. In 2004 for instance Scott Bradfield lamented the fact that *Beloved* had become an apparently sacred book that it is almost impossible to criticise without being accused of racism and sexism. For him *Beloved* has a self-righteous, holier-than-thou feel that is difficult to tolerate.[1] However, a much higher profile dissenting voice comes from Harold Bloom who, while regarding Morrison as a genius, does not feel that *Beloved* is her best work. For Bloom, 'It is a narrative intended to shock us into ideological awareness, but its contrivances of plot are tendentious, and the personalities of its protagonists do not always cohere.'[2] While Bloom fails to unpack his criticisms, a more developed attack came from the poet and cultural commentator, Stanley Crouch in his 1987 review, and this is worth discussing this in more detail here.

Stanley Crouch argues that the African American novelist James Baldwin (1924–1987) created a fashion for suffering in American culture that has negatively affected African American writing. There was a time when tragedy and suffering seemed to be at odds with American optimism—to use Crouch's words, 'Americans hate los-

---

1   Scott Bradfield 'Why I Hate Toni Morrison's *Beloved*,' *Denver Quarterly* 38.4 (2004): 86–99.
2   'Introduction,' Bloom, Harold (ed). *Toni Morrison* (Philadelphia: Chelsea House Publishers, 2002) 1

ers'[1]—but now misery and catastrophe occupy a central role in enter-
tainment: writers who dwell on such issues are less prone to accusations of self-pity. According to Crouch this has developed into a
tendency for African American women to be presented as quintes-
sential figures of oppression, both in relation to white and black men.
He cites writers like Alice Walker as being among those who wallow
in the misery of black women, and produce work characterised by:
'melodrama, militant self-pitying, guilt-mongering, and pretentions
to mystic wisdom' [Crouch, 66]. He accuses Morrison of cashing
in on this fashion in her role as editor at Random House where she
actively championed black female writers. He also criticises her
for not doing enough to distance herself from some of the hostile,
racist rhetoric associated with the more militant black activists in the
1960s. Though he concedes that, 'unlike Alice Walker,' Morrison has
'real talent,' he criticises *Beloved* on a number of grounds. Firstly he
attacks Morrison for comparing the 'Sixty Million and more' who
died in the Middle Passage to the victims of the Holocaust; he feels
that she tried to create a 'blackface Holocaust novel,' without the req-
uisite talent for rendering tragedy. He accuses Morrison of simplify-
ing the issues and omitting reference to the involvement of Africans
in the enslavement of their own people, such as those who captured
their enemies and sold them to white slavetraders. She presents slavery solely in terms of white injustice to black people and denies the
complexity of the issue. Crouch also accuses her of proselytising in
her work, ineptly weaving ideological statements into her narrative,
and creating characters that are merely vehicles for her reductive
message:

> As in all protest pulp fiction, everything is locked into its own
> time, and is ever the result of external social forces. We learn
> little about the souls of human beings, we are only told what
> will happen if they are treated very badly. The world exists
> in a purple haze of overstatement, of false voices, of strained
> homilies; nothing very subtle is ever really tried. *Beloved* reads
> largely like a melodrama lashed to the structural conceits of the

---

1   Stanley Crouch 'Aunt Medea,' *Critical Essays on Toni Morrison's* Beloved. (New
York: G.K. Hall & Co, 1998) 64–71.

miniseries [Crouch, 68]

Among the stock scenes that Crouch feels Morrison includes for effect are the 'obligatory moment of transcendent female solidarity' where Amy helps Sethe give birth, and the depictions of sexual exploitation; such prefabricated moments are facile and predictable. Ultimately Crouch feels that she fails to capture the 'ambiguities of the human soul which transcend race' and as a result produces a contrived and reductive book. Morrison's world is too morally black and white, then, and she exploits fashion and prejudice to make a political point.

Several commentators have implied that Crouch's critique seems born of a cultural anxiety about black women rather than a genuine attempt to evaluate the book. Others have drawn attention to the essentialist thinking unpinning his notions of the 'human soul' and 'human spirit', concepts that existed alongside slavery and the Holocaust; as Paul Gilroy suggests, they are indicative of 'the ideologies of humanism with which those brutal histories can be shown to have been complicit'[1] and are thus indicative of reductive and reactionary thinking on Crouch's part, rather than Morrison's

5.6 Beloved the Film

Oprah Winfrey's company Harpo Productions purchased the film rights to Morrison's novel almost immediately after its publication, and the film eventually appeared in 1998 directed by Jonathan Demme. It stared Winfrey herself as Sethe, Danny Glover as Paul D., Beah Richards as Baby Suggs, Kimberly Elise as Denver, and Thandie Newton as Beloved. The reviews were mixed and the film did not do well commercially. It received one Oscar nomination for costume design, and some of the actors, most notably Kimberly Elise, received praise and nominations for minor awards; essentially the critical response fell way short of expectations given the success of the source novel. The depiction of Beloved is particularly problematic. Thandie Newton is a British actress and there was some

---

1   Quoted in Carl Plasa (ed) *Toni Morrison,* Beloved: *A Reader's Guide to Essential Criticism.* (Cambridge: Icon Books, 2000) 31

criticism that she was not portrayed by an African American; more importantly the performance itself was criticised:

> Whereas Morrison created a feral but relatively articulate person [...] the film presents a repulsive creature (a bizarre performance by Thandie Newton) whose croaks and drools and screeches recalls Linda Blair's demonic child in the exorcist.[1]

It is difficult to relate to this character in any way other than as a grotesque, and all of the subtlety and nuance of Beloved's character as she appears in the novel is lost. The story is essentially reduced to a simple ghost story with no room for alternative readings of Beloved's character. There is no reference to the Middle Passage, for instance, which is absolutely crucial for linking her character to general African American history, nor is there any suggestion that Beloved might be an escaped sex slave, so an alternative non-supernatural reading is also largely precluded.

For the most part the action of the film is centred on 124, and there are very few references to Sweet Home. As a result the significance of the slave experience and its relevance to the central story is undermined. Also the issue of masculinity and the unmanning consequences of slavery are absent: Paul D's demeaning experiences on the chain gang are excluded, for instance, and this undermines his potential significance as a character; Beloved's sexual relationship with Paul D is retained but it is difficult to see the point of this outside the context of Paul's broader life. In the novel she acts as a catalyst for his memory too, but this doesn't work in the film because we don't get a sense of what Paul has repressed. The more peripheral male characters are only briefly mentioned, and this is also a huge omission, particularly in the case of Sixo: his irrepressible spirit and determination both in his role as a lover of the Thirty Mile Woman, and in his defiance of schoolteacher, makes an important statement about humanity's capacity for resistance. In the novel this is reinforced with Sixo's celebration of 'Seven–o' in the final moments of his life, suggesting the enduring nature of such spirit, and of African American people in general.

---

1   John C Tibbetts 'Oprah's Belabored Beloved', Literature/Film Quarterly; 1999; 27, 1, 74

The film ends, not as in the novel with an assertion of Beloved's ambiguity, but with a section from Baby Suggs's speech from chapter nine. She addresses a group of black people in the Clearing, telling them that they must love themselves: their skins and their hearts. The scene is repositioned to follow that in which Paul D tells Sethe that she is her own 'best thing' and she answers, 'Me? Me?' This repositioning *does* serve to create a degree of closure for the movie: Baby Suggs's words make general Paul D's specific statement about self-love: his point that Sethe must respect and value herself is made to apply to all black people. While this gives the film some shape, almost all of the subtlety of the novel is lost and the former has little of the latter's complexity or force.

6. Selected Bibliography

6.1 Works on Beloved

Andrews, William L. & McKay, Nellie. *Beloved: A Casebook* (Oxford: Oxford University Press, 1999). This includes some notable historical documents such as a contemporary review of the Margaret Garner incident written by an abolitionist, and a poem by Frances Ellen Watkins Harper written at the time of the killing. Among the excellent critical essays is one by Linda Krumholz addressing ritual in *Beloved*, and another on postmodernism and the problems of representing black identity in *Beloved*, written by Rafael Perez-Torres. The book closes with a conversation on the novel by three critics each offering different responses to various aspects of the book.

Solomon, Barbara H. *Critical Essays on Toni Morrison's* Beloved. (New York: G.K. Hall & Co, 1998). This collects together some of the most important reviews and articles on *Beloved* to have appeared up to the nineties. They include reviews from Margaret Atwood and Walter Clemons, together with Stanley Crouch's hostile reading. It also offers essays on the politics of identity in the text, *Beloved* and the oral tradition, the question of possession, time in *Beloved*, and the issue of memory in the novel.

Tally, Justine. *Toni Morrison's* Beloved*: Origins* (New York: Routledge, 2009). This discusses what the author sees as the artistic use of Michel Foucault's theories in *Beloved*. Tally explores the origins of the story—i.e. the sources it appears to reference— and finds that they go beyond African culture, extending to Greek mythology. She argues that Morrison's text constitutes an intentional corrective to Enlightenment philosophy, challenging traditional conceptions of motherhood. The book is interesting because of the close attention it gives to certain aspects of the novel, and original readings of some characters and episodes: for instance, it speculates whether Amy Denver might be a ghost brought forth by the yet-to-be-born Denver, or that she might herself be of African descent: in other words Tally challenges the idea that Amy is included to suggest the possibility of black and white collaboration and harmony.

6.2 Works on Toni Morrison

Tally, Justine (ed). *The Cambridge Companion to TonI Morrison.* (Cambridge: Cambridge University Press, 2007). This collection contains essays on all of Morrison's novels up to *Love*, and also includes scholarly work on her short stories, and literary and social criticism. There is an article on memory in *Beloved* by Claudine Raynaud, and a piece discussing *Beloved* as a trilogy alongside *Jazz* and *Paradise*.

Peterson, Nancy J. (ed.) Toni Morrison: Critical and Theoretical Approaches (Baltimore: John Hopkins University Press, 1997). This collects articles on Morrison that have appeared in Modern Fiction Studies, a double issue of which focused exclusively on Morrison in 1993. Part One collects three black feminist critiques, Part Two discusses Morrison in relation to postmodernism, Part Three looks at Morrison's works as 'cultural interventions,' and Part Four includes reader and writer responses, together with the author's own Nobel Prize speech.

Denard, C. Carolyn (ed). *Toni Morrison: Conversations.* (Mississippi: University Press of Mississippi, 2008). This includes many of the important interviews from 1976 to 2005, presented chronologically. *Beloved* is mentioned in almost all of the post-1987 interviews of course. The first part of the book is particularly useful in helping to develop sense of Morrison's motivation and background as a writer, while the second part focuses more on text-specific interviews. Among the more substantial and significant interviews is the one she gave in the Art of Fiction series for *The Paris Review* in 1992.

6.3 Internet Sources

The Toni Morrison Society. This was founded 1993 and publishes a newsletter, *Wordwork*, and an annual bibliography of scholarship. They also hold Morrison related events throughout the year including symposia, conferences, lecture series, and prizes.

http://www.tonimorrisonsociety.org/index.html

Toni Morrison: 'I want to feel what I feel. Even if it's not happiness' Interview with Emma Brockes. *The Guardian*, Friday 13 April 2012. This interview was conducted on the publication of *Home*, but Morrison talks generally about her life and her work and this is a very interesting recent interview.

http://www.guardian.co.uk/books/2012/apr/13/
toni–morrison–home–son–love#

Toni Morrison. Unspeakable Things Unspoken: The Afro-American Presence in American Literature. The Tanner Lecture on Human Values, delivered at The University of Michigan October 7, 1988. This is a lecture in which Morrison discusses the relationship between African American literature and the American literary canon. She spends some time discussing her own books up to 1988, including *Beloved*.

http://tannerlectures.utah.edu/_documents/a-to-z/m/morrison90.
pdf

Toni Morrison, The Art of Fiction No. 134. *The Paris Review* Interview with Elissa Schappell. This is one of the most substantial interviews with Morrison and it is available for free here. She talks extensively about her influences, and makes many fascinating specific points about *Beloved*.

http://www.theparisreview.org/interviews/1888/
the-art-of-fiction-no-134-toni-morrison

Character List

Sethe

Sethe (pronounced Seth—uh) is an ex-slave of the Sweet Home plantation, wife of Halle and daughter-in-law of Baby Suggs. She attempted to murder her four children Buglar, Howard, Denver, and Beloved, in order to avoid having them taken in to slavery, but only succeeded in killing Beloved. She resides at 124 Bluestone Road in Cincinnati and is seemingly haunted by the ghost of her murdered child. She is also haunted by the trauma of her experiences as a slave, and at the start of the novel there is much she is trying to repress. She is a fiercely independent woman but the guilt she feels over her actions, together with the psychological pain associated with her slave history, have left her vulnerable and in denial about the past. When Paul D arrives at 124 he offers hope for the future but this is undermined with the arrival Beloved who Sethe later sees as a reincarnation of her murdered daughter.

Beloved

The name of a young woman who arrives at Bluestone Road eighteen years after Sethe's daughter (also called Beloved) was murdered. The implication is that she is a reincarnation of Sethe's daughter, although this is never confirmed; indeed, there is also evidence to suggest that she could be an escaped sex-slave completely unrelated to Sethe. Either way she has an otherworldly quality and acts as a catalyst for change for several characters in the novel, most notably Sethe, Denver, and Paul D. In a broader sense she represents the return of the painful past for African Americans: the traumatic history of slavery which they struggle to come to terms with.

Denver

Sethe's daughter, born while Sethe was in the process of fleeing Sweet Home: midway between slavery and freedom. She is named after Amy Denver, the young white girl who assisted Sethe in the delivery. She is lonely at Bluestone Road and gravitates toward Beloved when she arrives. Initially fearful of her mother, Denver comes to understand more about her in the latter stages of the novel. She is seen to mature as it progresses and at the close this former recluse is able to move into the community as a viable sociable being. Intelligent and outward-looking, she comes to represent a positive future for the next generation of African Americans.

Paul D

The last surviving male slave from Sweet Home. He knew Sethe when she was a slave and desired her. Like Sethe he is also struggling to come to terms with his past and the brutality he experienced both as a slave and as a prisoner on a chain-gang; he keeps his feelings metaphorically buried in a rusty tobacco tin, and throughout the book is troubled by insecurities about his self-worth and masculinity. On escaping prison he spent many years wandering until arriving at 124 and becoming Sethe's lover. His past life makes him wary of investing emotionally in relationships, but his connection with Sethe helps him develop as a person and his willingness to commit to her reveals his capacity for love.

Baby Suggs (aka Grandma Baby)

Mother of Halle and mother-in-law of Sethe, Baby Suggs moves to 124 Bluestone Road when she is bought out of slavery by her son, Halle. She has an affinity with the spiritual world and is a gifted preacher who regularly address the community at a place called the Clearing. Sethe sends her three children to 124 ahead of her attempt to flee Sweet Home, and Baby looks after them until Sethe arrives. Following Sethe's attempts to murder her children Baby retreats to her bed and dies; she becomes disillusioned with the world, blaming white people for the suffering of blacks, and feeling helpless in the face their power and inhumanity. She is, however, an inspirational figure and her influence pervades the novel, affecting the lives of Sethe, Denver, and other members of the African American community years after her death.

Schoolteacher

The man who takes charge of Sweet Home after Mr Garner's death. The husband of Mrs Garner's late sister, he introduces a harsh regime at the plantation, effectively treating slaves like animals. He uses the language of science to assert the inferiority of black people and what he perceives as their sub-human status. Throughout the novel his name is spelt with a lower case s which works to qualify his assumptions about his elevated station.

Stamp Paid

The man who helps Sethe and Denver in their escape from Sweet Home. A member of the Underground Railroad during the years of slavery, he remains a pillar of the black community in Cincinnati and has devoted his life to helping black people. He was married to a woman called Vashti who was forced to have sex with a slave holder's son. Stamp's restraint on learning of this and not killing either his wife or her abuser made him change his name from Joshua to Stamp Paid: it refers to his sense of having paid his moral and emotional debt to the world.

Amy Denver

A white indentured servant girl who assists Sethe in giving birth to Denver, and after whom Sethe names her daughter. She too is a runaway, and some critics see her as the novel's attempt to remind readers that not all white people are wicked.

Halle Suggs

Sethe's husband and the youngest of Baby Suggs' eight sons. During his years as a slave on Sweet Home he worked in his free time to pay for his mother's freedom. When he witnesses Sethe's brutalisation at the hands of schoolteacher's nephews he goes insane: Paul D is the last of the Sweet Home characters to see him and he is assumed dead by the time the story begins.

Sixo

A courageous and rebellious Sweet Home slave, Sixo retains a degree of independence by wandering around at night, dancing, and maintaining a relationship with a woman called Patsy, even though it is a thirty mile journey to see her. Through her he discovers the Underground Railroad and the possibility of escape from Sweet Home. When he is caught schoolteacher burns him alive, but he dies courageously laughing, singing, and shouting about his unborn son, Seven-O, who seems destined to escape slavery with Patsy.

Mr. and Mrs. Garner

The owners of Sweet Home are an ostensibly benign and caring couple who treat the slaves comparatively well. However, the novel makes the point that that their paternalism is as unjust as schoolteacher's brutal racism, and merely supports the same dangerous ideology.

Lady Jones

A black teacher who runs a school for underprivileged black children near to 124 Bluestone Road. She hates her light skin colour and blonde hair because she feels estranged by her mixed race heritage. Denver attended her school for a while when she was young and seeks her help when Beloved takes over the house. Lady Jones assists her, galvanizing the community who begin to provide food aid for the family. She becomes Denver's mentor and friend and represents the possible future that education might provide for African American women.

Ella

A woman who worked with Stamp Paid on the Underground Railroad. She was brutalized by a white father and son who kept her captive to use as a sex slave. As a woman with a traumatic past, she can identify with Sethe and when she learns of her predicament she organises the women of the community to exorcise Beloved from 124.

Mr. and Miss Bodwin

This brother and sister couple are white abolitionists who helped Sethe when she murdered Beloved. Though ostensibly liberal and caring individuals, certain aspects of their views and lifestyle make us uncomfortable. They are a little condescending to black people, and when Denver visits their house she sees that they own a slave figurine depicting the words: 'At Yo' Service.' Despite their good intentions, the latter suggests a degree of complicity with the kind of thinking that produced slavery.

Paul F and Paul A

The two other Pauls who work at Sweet Home alongside their brother, Paul D. Following her husband's death, Mrs. Garner sells Paul F, while Paul A is hanged by schoolteacher following the failed escape attempt from the plantation.

Buglar and Howard

Sethe's sons who run away from 124. Early in the novel it suggested that they flee because they are afraid of the ghost that haunts the house, however some critics feel that another motive for their departure might be a fear of Sethe and the possibility that she might try to kill them again. Sethe later has dreams of her boys walking away from her, deaf to her calls for them to return.

Nan

A one-armed slave woman whose job it was to nurse the children of slaveholders and the slaves. She cares for Sethe when she is little, telling her stories of her mother who was on the same slave ship as her on the Middle Passage journey from Africa.

Sethe's Mother

The reader never learns Sethe's mother's name. She endured the Middle Passage from Africa with Nan, and was raped repeatedly during the journey. She disposed of all the unwanted children apart from Sethe whom she kept because she had felt an attachment to her father. She dies by hanging, and her body is left to rot on the rope, a memory that Sethe represses until the arrival of Beloved.

A Note on the Author

Paul McDonald works at the University of Wolverhampton where he is Senior Lecturer in American Literature and Course Leader for Creative Writing. He is the author of thirteen books, including three poetry collections and three novels. His criticism includes books on Philip Roth, the fiction of the Industrial Midlands, and postmodern American fiction.

Humanities-Ebooks.co.uk

All Humanities Ebooks titles are available to Libraries through EBSCO and MyiLibrary.com

Some Academic titles

Sibylle Baumbach, *Shakespeare and the Art of Physiognomy*
John Beer, *Blake's Humanism*
John Beer, *The Achievement of E M Forster*
John Beer, *Coleridge the Visionary*
Jared Curtis, ed., *The Fenwick Notes of William Wordsworth**
Jared Curtis, ed., *The Cornell Wordsworth: A Supplement**
Steven Duncan, *Analytic Philosophy of Religion: its History since 1955**
John K Hale, *Milton as Multilingual: Selected Essays 1982–2004*
Simon Hull, ed., *The British Periodical Text, 1797–1835*
Rob Johnson, Mark Levene and Penny Roberts, eds., *History at the End of the World* *
John Lennard, *Modern Dragons and other Essays on Genre Fiction**
C W R D Moseley, *Shakespeare's History Plays*
Paul McDonald, *Laughing at the Darkness: Postmodernism and American Humour* *
Colin Nicholson, *Fivefathers: Interviews with late Twentieth-Century Scottish Poets*
W J B Owen, *Understanding 'The Prelude'*
Pamela Perkins, ed., *Francis Jeffrey's Highland and Continental Tours**
Keith Sagar, *D. H. Lawrence: Poet**
Reinaldo Francisco Silva, *Portuguese American Literature**
William Wordsworth, *Concerning the Convention of Cintra**
W J B Owen and J W Smyser, eds., *Wordsworth's Political Writings**
The Poems of William Wordsworth: Collected Reading Texts from the Cornell Wordsworth, 3 vols.*

* These titles are also available in print using links from
http://www.humanities-ebooks.co.uk

Humanities Insights

These are some of the Insights available at:
http://www.humanities-ebooks.co.uk/

General Titles

An Introduction to Critical Theory
Modern Feminist Theory
An Introduction to Rhetorical Terms

Genre FictionSightlines

Octavia E Butler: *Xenogenesis / Lilith's Brood*
Reginal Hill: *On Beulah's Height*
Ian McDonald: *Chaga / Evolution's Store*
Walter Mosley: *Devil in a Blue Dress*
Tamora Pierce: *The Immortals*
Tamora Pierce: *Protectr of the Small*

History Insights

Oliver Cromwell
The British Empire: Pomp, Power and Postcolonialism
The Holocaust: Events, Motives, Legacy
Lenin's Revolution
Methodism and Society
The Risorgimento

Literature Insights

Austen: *Emma*
Conrad: *The Secret Agent*
T S Eliot: 'The Love Song of J Alfred Prufrock' and *The Waste Land*
English Renaissance Drama: Theatre and Theatres in Shakespeare's Time
Faulkner: *Go Down, Moses* and *Big Woods'*
Faulkner: *The Sound and the Fury*
Gaskell, *Mary Barton*
Hardy: *Tess of the Durbervilles*
Heller: *Catch-22*
Ibsen: *The Doll's House*
Hopkins: Selected Poems
Hughes: *New Selected Poems*
Larkin: *Selected Poems*
Lawrence: Selected Short Stories
Lawrence: *Sons and Lovers*
Lawrence: *Women in Love*

Paul Scott: *The Raj Quartet*
Shakespeare: *Hamlet*
Shakespeare: *Henry IV*
Shakespeare: *King Lear*
Shakespeare: *Richard II*
Shakespeare: *Richard III*
Shakespeare: *The Merchant of Venice*
Shakespeare: *The Tempest*
Shakespeare: *Troilus and Cressida*
Shelley: *Frankenstein*
Wordsworth: *Lyrical Ballads*
Fields of Agony: English Poetry and the First World War

Philosophy Insights

American Pragmatism
Barthes
Thinking Ethically about Business
Critical Thinking
Existentialism
Formal Logic
Metaethics
Contemporary Philosophy of Religion
Philosophy of Sport
Plato
Wittgenstein
Žižek

Some Titles in Preparation

Aesthetics
Philosophy of Language
Philosophy of Mind
Political Psychology
Plato's *Republic*
Renaissance Philosophy
Rousseau's legacy

Austen: *Pride and Prejudice*
Blake: *Songs of Innocence & Experience*
Chatwin: *In Patagonia*
Dreiser: *Sister Carrie*
Eliot, George: *Silas Marner*
Eliot: *Four Quartets*
Fitzgerald: *The Great Gatsby*
Hardy: Selected Poems
Heaney: Selected Poems
James: *The Ambassadors*
Lawrence: *The Rainbow*
Melville: *Moby-Dick*
Melville: Three Novellas
Shakespeare: *Macbeth*
Shakespeare: *Romeo and Juliet*
Shakespeare: *Twelfth Night*

CPSIA information can be obtained
at www.ICGtesting.com
Printed in the USA
LVHW020110090819
627063LV00001B/85/P